Helen Heritage is a Melbourne writer. She is the author of a short story collection, *The Messenger*, and her work has appeared in a number of journals including *Meanjin*, *Overland* and *Westerley*. In 2007 she was one of the winners of La Mama's First Time Playwrights prize, and her play, *The Devil's Dictionary*, was performed at the theatre/gallery fortyfivedownstairs. She has taught writing at the Centre for Adult Education (CAE) in Melbourne and has written reviews for Australian Book Review.

BORROWED LANDSCAPE

Helen Heritage

Waxflower Press Melbourne Australia

In memory of my mother

and

for Peter

Friends part
forever – wild geese
lost in cloud.

(Matsuo Basho 1644–94)

I still dream about Hanaka. Even after fifty years. In this dream, Hanaka and I are in a garden, a Japanese landscape garden with a tea house beyond a lake. I hear Hanaka laugh but I cannot see her, cannot reach her, although I yearn to do so.

Every time I have this dream my heart breaks all over again, just as it was broken when I was a girl of fourteen. I wake up crying out to Hanaka from my deepest self: *Why did you disappear forever from my life?*

Part One

1

The Pacific War ruined my family as effectively as a dropped bomb, so Aunt Maggie always said. My father went to war when I was a baby of nine months and he returned in 1946 when I was six years old. He returned a ruined man, ruined, according to Maggie, because of the Japanese. The ill, thin man who was Jack my father was not the handsome man in uniform smiling out from the silver frame on my grandmother's chiffonier and so I understood that ruin was when you became someone different from what you once were, but different in a heartbreaking way.

Although our house may have once sung with children wildly pulling each other on rugs along the wooden floorboards and where one year, I was told, a small guest vomited spectacularly over the two-bar radiator after gorging an entire cake; sung with hissing cats and a barking dog all dressed in old baby clothes for an impromptu pet show, the memory of which still made my mother laugh – I couldn't remember those times. Rather, our house was a place where, when my father wasn't 'well', we all tiptoed and tried not to bang doors; a place where something bad could happen at any time and where sometimes the silence was like very deep water and I knew that if I wasn't careful I might be pulled under and drowned.

The first time you see a man cry, it's a tremendous shock; but when that man is your father, something inside you changes forever. I remember clearly the first time I saw my father cry – great gulping sobs, mucus running from his nose – he couldn't stop even though he tried when he saw me, my mother's face anguished as she hurried him into their bedroom and shut the door. What was wrong? What had happened in the war that made him cry like that? The only explanation Mum gave was that 'something bad' had happened in New Guinea. Once during one of my father's nightmares, I heard him call a name. 'Who's Danny?' I asked Mum a few days later. She didn't want to answer but I persisted.

'A friend of Dad's, a young boy, who died.' I suspected my mother knew a lot more of the story but she clearly wasn't going to tell it to me.

My father had been sick since he came back from the war – he'd had malaria and malnutrition – but at first Mum thought he'd be alright in time. He didn't eat much and either had insomnia or nightmares but then he started drinking and would get angry and shout at us, which frightened my little brother, Johnno, as well as me and my mother. He'd lost his job in an accounting firm – he couldn't concentrate and so couldn't do the work required of him – and this became a pattern. Eventually he had to go to the Repatriation Hospital in Heidelberg for treatment, the first of many admissions: it was as if our father rode around and around on some ghastly carousel which he could never get off, while we, his hapless family, waited for the carousel to slow down and let the man he once was return to us.

It wasn't until I was about nine that I realised my father's illness was one of the mind and I learned never to talk about it to strangers. If someone asked, you said he had pneumonia or a heart condition, even leprosy was better than 'war neurosis', as many people thought men who had war neurosis were weak and cowardly, even the Government who denied him a full pension because they wanted proof that the psychological damage occurred *solely* because of the war experience.

A famous American general in the war, General Patton, was demoted for slapping a serviceman and calling him a coward while the man was in hospital suffering a mental breakdown. If even General Patton thought like that, my grandmother said, families like ours were really up against it, no matter that my father had been awarded a medal for bravery.

My family consisted of my mother and father, younger brother, Johnno, and our Aunt Maggie who was Dad's sister. We lived in a large Victorian house that had belonged to Dad and Maggie's parents who'd left it to them both. They'd left all their belongings too, and sometimes I thought it peculiar that we lived surrounded by dead people's furniture, crockery, bibs and bobs, even their clothes still packed away in cupboards. Both Dad and Maggie were extremely attached to the house and although Mum would have liked to have her own house, the truth was, with Dad being sick, the money Maggie paid toward the groceries and upkeep of the house, as well as her help when my father was at his worst, helped keep things afloat. However, Maggie could be difficult – argumentative and sarcastic as well as loud and untidy – and often Mum commented that she wished Maggie would get married, perhaps then she'd leave the house. But, as I reminded her, Maggie might bring her new husband home to live with us.

Maggie and I didn't much care for one another, but I was careful not to antagonise her as she had a short fuse. She was the adult, Mum said, and until I was old enough, I should do as she said. However, Mum made it quite clear that Maggie was not the one to punish Johnno or me for any wrongdoing.

My mother and Maggie were chalk and cheese – both in nature and in looks. Where Mum was lady-like and gentle, Maggie was all hot air and loud laughter, enjoying a drink and a coarse joke. Yet she loved her brother and, when he was at his worst, which for us was when he was raging, it was Maggie who could quieten him, sometimes with a sharp command, sometimes by leading him to the back verandah where she'd give him his pipe and talk quietly to him as they both smoked. Dad and Maggie even looked alike – both had light brown hair and blue eyes – whereas Mum and Johnno had dark curly hair and brown eyes with dark, thick eyelashes. I wasn't like anyone else in the family, having dark but straight hair and hazel eyes with ordinary sort of lashes.

While Maggie's hot-air nature seemed to help keep her in rude good health, my mother's natural constraint made her drawn and anxious. I resented this. Sometimes it seemed that Maggie was sucking the life out of my mother; certainly my father was. If only Mum was more ... more *vigorous*, but as it was, my mother often seemed to be way out of her depth.

2

Aunt Maggie was a great hater, and she hated the Japanese more than anything else. It was a hatred of such intensity that we were all swept up in it. She had cause, I don't deny, what with my father and, my mother whispered, a good friend who'd been killed in New Guinea. Brothers of friends, friends of my father's, one of our cousins, the stories of horror at the hands of an enemy deemed dishonourable seemed without end. 'Monsters', 'barbarians', 'yellow devils' were terms I heard often as I grew up. Generally speaking, we didn't disagree, but we were trying to get on, to put it behind us, and Maggie's obsession was damaging all of us. My mother, who hated conflict, tried to put a stop to it. It was bad for Jack's recovery, she'd tell Maggie, and very bad for the children, especially Johnno. He was a sweet, nervous boy who'd developed what the doctor called 'nervous asthma'.

'What good can it do? The past can't be changed. You must stop this!'

But Maggie was not going to be told what to do by my mother. Her tirades continued and we each developed ploys to get away from her when she began to 'hold forth'. While the rest of the world was racing to put the Second World War way behind it, my family couldn't, because in a sense we were still living it, and Maggie's ugly obsession dragged us down further. Her hatred was further fed when the servicemen who had married Japanese women during the Allied Occupation of

Japan wanted to bring their wives back to Australia. Maggie wasn't the only Australian who objected to this but the most important one, the Minister for Immigration, Arthur Calwell, was the one she liked to quote. We got tired of hearing Calwell's words: 'It would be the grossest act of public indecency to permit a Japanese of either sex to pollute Australian or Australian-controlled shores.' Maggie called these women 'harlots' and the men who wanted to marry them 'deviants' and 'a bloody disgrace to their country'. But despite Maggie and Arthur Calwell, the first Japanese war bride, Cherry Parker, had arrived in Australia in 1952 and her picture was in all the papers.

'Bold as brass! Walking down the street as if she owned the joint!' Maggie burst through the front door one late afternoon. She had spied a woman she took to be a Japanese war bride in our quiet leafy suburb. Even my father, going through a good phase which gave us hope, told her to 'put a lid on it!'

'All I'm saying is, she'd better not come near me! I'll tell her exactly what I think of her and her yellow race!'

'What's she look like?' Johnno's eyes were wide at the thought of a yellow person. My mother cut in. 'She's an Asian person, a bit like Mr Lim.'

'But he's not yellow,' Johnno said.

Wrinkled Mr Lim with hardly any teeth? I was sure she looked a lot better than that!

'Remember, you two, I will not tolerate rudeness or unkindness.'

Maggie lit a Turf. Mum hated her smoking at the dinner table. 'What about me, Kitty?'

'Clear the table, please, Louise. Johnno, go and water my hydrangeas, there's a love ... they'll be drooping.'

'You haven't answered me, Kitty.'

'I hold no sway over you, Maggie.'

'Ha! Next, you'll be bringing out Mum's Royal Doulton and inviting Tokyo Rose to tea!'

Maggie needn't have worried because, although my mother might wish us not to be unkind to the 'war bride', make no mistake, neither would she ever have entertained the idea of any of us becoming friendly with this woman. My mother didn't blame the woman personally, but it was this woman's people who had ruined my father – we all understood that.

Despite our feelings towards the Japanese – we didn't much care for the Germans either – my mother and I were especially interested in other cultures. We may not have met many of these different people, but we certainly loved reading about them. The family myth was that from the age of six, I could read *The Argus* newspaper from cover to cover. That was a slight exaggeration but when reports came out revealing the existence of the concentration camps, Auschwitz and Dachau and others, my mother told me she'd wept and hid the papers from me just in case. The second family myth, which had much more truth in it, was that I listened to everything and so was what my grandmother called, 'rather advanced'. It was a quality that seemed to make my family proud but, at the same time, gave them some unease. I couldn't help that I was wise beyond my years.

Every second Saturday, the man we called the Library Man came to our house carrying his well-worn books in two battered brown suitcases. His name was Mr McCabe, and he always wore a grey dustcoat over his clothes. Although he tipped his hat to my mother when he entered the house, he never took it off. After my first period when I was twelve, my mother ceased her attempts – usually unsuccessful – at censoring what I read, hence my worldly education really began. I learnt about injustice: *Of Mice and Men* and *The Good Earth* were two favourites. I learnt too about sex – not so much its anatomical details, which I knew about but could never imagine anyone *actually* doing – but about passion. I might not understand exactly what Maria meant in Hemingway's *For Whom the Bell Tolls* when she asked, 'Did the earth never move for thee before?' but I did understand clearly that it was something very good indeed! I adored

Scarlett O'Hara in *Gone with the Wind* and almost equally adored the nobler, but less beautiful, Melanie. I ploughed my way through Graham Greene, but he was way above my head.

Although my mother shared my love of reading, she read, not as I did to learn what a life, *my* life, could possibly become, but as an escape *from* her own life which was, I understood, slightly different *to* escaping into someone else's life. My father's illness, his unpredictable drinking, the inescapable fact of sharing the house with the rumbustious Maggie and my brother's asthma, all eroded my gentle-natured mother. She seemed constantly on edge, as if expecting some disaster or other. The only time my mother was at total ease was when she was deep in a book, her feet tucked under her, a cup of tea by her side.

3

It was one hot endless day during the school holidays, while playing 'run through the hose' with Johnno and longing for my friend Libby to come home from the beach that I first saw the Japanese war bride. She was walking up our street holding an opened umbrella and wearing a white cotton dress printed with red roses, a shopping basket over one arm. Her straight black hair gleamed. I stared and, seeing my stare, she smiled in an unsure way as if not quite knowing how to translate it. Quickly, not so much remembering my manners as knowing I really wanted to speak to her, I said hello, and her smile became more certain. She was incredibly strange and beautiful. She did not look like 'the grossest act of public indecency' to me. The woman said hello to me and continued up our street.

Nearly everyone I knew was Australian-born, mainly from Anglo-Celtic stock. A family up our street who'd migrated from London immediately after the war were considered almost exotic. The first Jew who I could clearly identify as such was the gaunt old man with a black skull cap who sold fabrics up the Spring Street end of Bourke Street. My mother and I went there to buy material for winter skirts because she was told he sold good quality at a cheap price. The shop was unlike any I had ever been into, with bolts and bolts of fabrics of all kinds seemingly thrown every which way and no care at all about how the window display looked. The man spoke with a thick accent, and was very brusque. I think the man and the

13

chaos in the shop unnerved my mother as we never went there again, although she did say to me, 'God knows what that man's been through.' The Italians too had begun to arrive in large numbers – Maggie called them 'Dagos' – and sometimes on a tram or train I saw old ladies dressed completely in black each with a gold cross around her neck. Once even, one such lady was fingering rosary beads. As well as the Italians, people from Eastern Europe began migrating to Australia. We all knew that foreign men were more hot-blooded and not as easily controlled as the native-born, and girls were warned to think carefully before agreeing to go out with them. A boy from Ukrainia, as I thought it was called, had come to my school. His name was Toluk and he was very handsome, did not speak any English and wore funny leather shorts with braces, which made me embarrassed for him.

The Woman's Page of *The Argus* newspaper printed 'This week's foreign recipe', which my mother always read, often shaking her head in doubt as to its edibility. Our greengrocer, Mr Lim, was Chinese and he and his family were the only Asian people I regularly saw except when we went to a Chinese restaurant in a country town or, rarely, to Little Bourke Street in the city. Mr Lim's grandfather had come to Australia during the Gold Rush.

From the first time I saw her, I was entranced by the Japanese war bride. Her exotic and tragic past, as I imagined it to be, and the romance of her love affair with an Australian soldier for whom she'd left her country, made her a heroine straight out of a novel. By stepping into our quiet suburban street, where nothing glamorous ever happened, she changed the possibilities of my world. I was determined to see her again.

The first day I walked to the shops without my mother-in-law, I saw only two people and one large ginger cat. If this were Kure, the place I came from, the streets would be filled with

14

dried fish and udon noodle sellers calling out their wares, shopgirls gossiping, housewives sprinkling salt and washing the entrance to their homes clean.

When I entered the butcher shop, the young man who helps the butcher, his apron smeared with blood, even a tiny piece of gristle, could not take his eyes from me. The same happened at the bakery, and even when I went into the haberdashery to buy cotton thread, I was aware of every eye on me. Worst of all was at the greengrocer where the old Chinaman stared at me in a horrible way. I walked home as quickly as I could and now I buy from the man who comes to my street once a week in his truck with vegetables fresh from the fields.

In Japan, I am like every other person. Here, I am someone very different. I do not like being one apart. Alan, my husband, said, 'Silly buggers. They'll get used to you.'

4

My plan was to wait for the war bride at the end of our street, then introduce myself and show her a shorter route to the shops. I didn't quite know what I'd do if she didn't understand me, but I reassured myself I could somehow mime my intentions. For two afternoons I waited, then changed to mornings. On the third morning, I saw her. Small and delicate, wearing a lemon skirt and white blouse and gloves, she was walking my way.

Her name was Hanaka, Hanaka McDonald. She spoke English well, which surprised me. I told her my name was Louise.

'Lou for short,' I said.

'The author of *Little Women* is Louisa May Alcott. That is Louise with the letter A instead of E, yes? I like this book very much.'

So began our friendship.

Although Hanaka looked very young, she was a married woman, so, although I longed to call her Hanaka, I knew I should address her as Mrs McDonald. I showed her the laneway at the back of the Presbyterian Church tennis courts. Her chance of meeting my angry aunt would be greatly lessened if she went that way, as would mine, but I didn't mention that. I bombarded her with silly questions: Did she like Melbourne? What about the food? Her house? She liked Australia very much; her mother-in-law was teaching her to cook; her house was very big and she was very lucky! This was not at all what I wanted. I wanted to know what she really thought! I tried a different tack.

'What Australian food do you hate?' I asked.

'Hate?'

'Something you don't like to eat.'

'My mother-in-law teaches me to cook the chump chop. But I don't like.'

'What did you eat in Japan? Is it true you eat raw fish?'

'*Sashimi* we call it. It is very good ... you like to try?'

'No! Thank you.'

'The fish must be fresh and healthy, and we add some sauce and a little paste that is hot in the mouth.'

I must have looked horrified, because Hanaka laughed, holding her hand over her mouth.

'For me, the chump chop is like the raw fish is for you,' she said. 'My mother-in-law also says I must learn to make parsley sauce. I try and try but ... Do you know this sauce? It is made with flour and milk and water from the vegetables.'

'My mother makes cheese sauce – I think it's the same except it's with cheese, not parsley.'

'You are lucky to have such a clever mother. '

'I'll ask her to show me ... then, if you like, I could show you ... '

Hanaka was delighted by my suggestion.

When I came to live in this suburb of the city of Melbourne, the space and the silence made me afraid, but I know now that inside these houses surrounded by large gardens and silent streets, women go about their daily tasks. I have taught myself to hear the sounds of life within this silence; a car starting up, the woman next door sweeping her front porch with a straw broom, a front gate opening across the road, sometimes in the still early morning, a rooster crowing. I have learned to gain comfort from the sound of the baker's cart, the greengrocer man, the milkman in the early morning. I like very much the sound of the horse clip-clopping slowly down the street, the clank of the milk bottles, then the milkman's commands to his horse.

I know I am lucky. I am never hungry and I live in my own large house which I am not quite used to yet, and although I do not always understand why he does certain things, my husband is very kind and loving. If I sometimes still yearn for the taste of my favourite pickle, or to meet Chie, my schooldays friend, in a tea house and chat with her about girlish things, or to go to the temple and pray, I know I must persevere and not let myself fall into melancholy. I am lucky.

5

Over the next few weeks, I learned that when I asked Hanaka a direct question, she often laughed and her response was clouded, unsatisfactory, but if I skirted around a topic, then slowly, slowly introduced what I wished to know, her answers were much more telling. In this way, I learnt she had met her husband, Alan, when she'd fallen during a storm and he'd picked her up, a fact I found suitably romantic; that he was an engineer who now worked for the State Electricity Department; and that the only family she had was an aunt and two cousins.

'Do they write to you?' I asked.

'My friend from school, Chie, writes to me sometimes,' Hanaka replied. From this, I deduced, her aunt and cousins did not. I wanted to know why, but knew it would be too rude to ask. Hanaka was especially curious about my mother. Did my mother wear slacks? Hanaka called them 'slack'. Gloves? Hat? When and where? Did lady friends come to tea? Did she cook fruit cake and roast lamb? Play Bridge? Read *The Women's Weekly*? Drink sherry? Strange questions, I thought, until I realised Hanaka was trying to learn how to be an Australian housewife.

One day, Hanaka brought up the subject of parsley sauce again. I'd forgotten all about it, and certainly hadn't learned how to make it.

'Mother McDonald, she says, "a roast is not complete without parsley sauce for the vegetables." ' I knew that Mother

McDonald was Hanaka's mother-in-law, and that Hanaka called her this ridiculous name because the woman had insisted.

Mother McDonald's opinion on parsley sauce was not the first I'd heard of her rigidly held views. She was sounding more and more like Maggie, except Maggie never cooked, and thankfully seemed not to care what she ate as long as there was plenty of it. Hanaka asked if I would help her and, wanting very much to both help as well as to see inside her house, I eagerly agreed.

That night, I asked Mum to teach me how to make white sauce the proper way. I'd often stirred the mixture while it thickened, and loved putting the grated cheese into the sauce, but Mum always started it and was responsible for the smooth finish.

'Why, Lou?' Mum was mystified. I told her we were doing sauces in Cooking and I wanted mine to be better than the teacher's pet, Julie Collins, who was a real pain. Mum taught me how to make a roux of the butter and flour and then to slowly blend the roux and liquid bit by bit before returning it to a low heat. I practised until I had it down pat.

When I first met Louise, I was so pleased to have someone to talk with, someone I could ask the many perplexing questions that filled my mind every day. To ask an older person, even my husband, would have made me embarrassed as some of these questions might seem quite foolish, but because Louise was still a schoolgirl, this was easier to do. Louise liked very much to tell me anything I asked. Once I asked her if her mother drank sherry. I know now that it was impolite to ask this, but Louise did not seem to think so. Louise told me her mother drinks sherry only on special occasions and, then, only one glass. Mother McDonald drinks sherry but my husband says she drinks too much sherry. So I now know that to drink sherry occasionally is correct, but to drink sherry more than

20

occasionally, especially every day before lunch and dinner and afterwards, as Mother McDonald does, is incorrect. What I do not understand is why Mother McDonald does not seem to care about her behaviour and why nobody corrects her.

Louise and I read The Women's Weekly *together every week and that is how I am learning to become an Australian housewife, although many things written in this magazine are hard for me to understand, such as that when Australian housewives are feeling 'nervy' they take medicine. Louise told me that 'nervy' means when a woman cannot look after her house properly and cries often. Sometimes such women, Louise said, 'take to the drink' but usually in secret so nobody knows. I have not found any articles in this magazine which tell me if it is correct for a woman to drink sherry at lunch and dinner. So I think Mother McDonald drinks too much sherry but not so much as to be said to be 'taking to the drink'.*

It is important for me to read The Women's Weekly *and I am lucky I have Louise to answer all my questions, but I am glad she likes to read books. A girl can learn more about the world through books than she can by reading about how to bake a certain cake or make a certain dress or to take a pill when one feels 'nervy'.*

6

Hanaka's house was a green weatherboard, not very old and lacking the charm of our Victorian-era house with its iron lacework, all the way around verandah and stained-glass window panels in red, amber and green patterned with birds and bell-shaped flowers.

Inside Hanaka's house, everything was so ordered it seemed empty and not at all welcoming, unlike my home, where the wicker basket sat piled with clean washing waiting to be ironed; where newspapers, books, empty teacups and cigarette butts in large ashtrays, as well as Johnno's cricket bat and stumps, which were supposed to live in the laundry, stayed where we left them until it was 'clean-up time' — in short, a house filled with the paraphernalia of five people, none of whom were tidy! Apart from a Japanese scroll on the wall of an alcove, and underneath, on a low table, a brown-glazed vase containing leaves and one dark red rose, nothing in the lounge-room made Hanaka's house different from any other.

Hanaka and I set to work and after I'd shown her exactly what Mum had showed me, we made and re-made the sauce at least six times. Finally, Hanaka did it all herself, adding the parsley at the end with satisfaction while I clapped and she bowed.

'Mother McDonald will be so pleased,' I told her.

I asked Hanaka if she wanted me to teach her how to make any other dishes.

'I already know how to make shepherd's pie and bread and butter pudding and trifle also.'

'Did Alan's mother teach you?'

'Women who were marrying Australian servicemen were given special classes on Australian life and food. We all thought bread and butter pudding very strange.'

How strange it was too, that although I knew these foods, had often eaten and enjoyed them, I didn't know how to cook them but Hanaka did!

In the cookery class we all laughed at the name 'shepherd's pie'. Some of us did not even know what a shepherd was – after all, there are no sheep in Japan. As for me, I could only imagine a shepherd of olden English times. I now know that, here, sheep are herded by dogs or men on horses. We were taught how to roast meat and potatoes and to make gravy to pour over this meat and that the correct thing to do with vegetables was to boil them until they were very soft. We made trifle, which I had read about in novels set in England, but we were not taught how to make Christmas pudding which, in my case, was perhaps wise. The first time I tasted this most traditional of English foods, one I had read about often, I felt immediately ill and had to rush from the room. My mother-in-law, Mother McDonald, was not pleased and my cheeks felt hot with shame but Alan, my husband, was very sympathetic, although afterwards, he did laugh. 'You should have seen Mum's face!' he said. Much later, he would joke that if I had been taught to make Christmas pudding in the cooking classes, I may never have married him.

None of the women in the class found the food we were taught to cook for our husbands to our taste. But we were all filled with an optimism sorely missing from our lives for so many years, so did not really understood that in our new country we would be required to cook these strange foods every day and eat them too. One woman, already the mother

23

of two sons by her husband and perhaps understanding what lay ahead for us better than myself and many others, told us not to worry, that all we needed to do to improve this food was to add pickles and soy sauce! Not one of us realised that the favourite pickles and sauces we used to enhance our food were not used in our new country, that even the rice would be a different type and that Australian housewives made rice pudding from it.

From the day I taught Hanaka how to make parsley sauce, I began to often go to her house. She let me call her Hanaka because she said I was like a little sister now but she always called me Louise, not Lou. I liked the way she said my name, more with an R than an L but not quite an R, sounding a bit, but not quite, like 'Roo-ees'. She told me that the letter L was hard for Japanese people to say. Hanaka asked me many questions about life as an Australian. She wanted to know about religion; did I have a religion, and did I practise it? When I told her we were Protestants, not Catholics, and that we didn't go to church at all, I wasn't quite truthful, because one Sunday just before Christmas the previous year, Mum had come into the kitchen wearing her best blue suit and holding a small black hat, handbag and gloves and announced that she was going to church.

'Can I come?' Johnno had asked. I had been too shocked to say anything.

'You'd be bored,' Mum had told Johnno.

And that had been that. From then on, each Sunday, the same ritual had occurred. Johnno had stopped asking after Mum explained he would have to sit perfectly still for a whole hour; he couldn't even cough.

'What if I wanted the lavatory?'

'Have to wait,' said Mum.

Was she going to become like old Mrs Box two doors away, who spoke of the Lord as if he were a close relation

24

living in the spare room? When I asked Mum this, she laughed and hugged me. She said her church-going was of a very different kind to Mrs Box's devotions. 'I like the peace,' she told me, which didn't really explain it satisfactorily.

'Couldn't you go into the garden for an hour and find the same kind of peace?' I asked her. Mum smiled and said no, that it wouldn't be the same.

Hanaka told me that in some parts of Japan, particularly in Nagasaki, there were many Christians, mainly Catholics. Wasn't Nagasaki one of the places where the atomic bomb was dropped? But I didn't say anything about that to Hanaka. I asked Mum later, and she said Nagasaki had been where the second bomb was dropped because the Emperor of Japan wouldn't surrender after Hiroshima was destroyed. 'I didn't know there were any Christians in Japan,' Mum said.

Hanaka said she was both a Buddhist and a follower of Shintoism, which was the religion of Japan before Buddhism spread from China. Shintoism was a religion where people prayed to spirits, she told me, the spirits of dead people or even the spirits in trees and rocks and mountains.

'It is so usual for we Japanese,' Hanaka said, 'to stop at a shrine going to or from work or on a holiday and ask the *kami* – the spirit – of that shrine to grant us luck in exams or in marriage or maybe when you wish to have a baby.'

Did Hanaka want to have a baby? I wondered who the baby would look like. Alan with his fair hair, or Hanaka? I hoped the baby would be a miniature Hanaka. Instead I said, 'I think Catholics do that, drop into Church to pray whenever they want to.'

7

One afternoon, Hanaka was unusually quiet. Was she sick, was she sad? Homesick? I knew I would have been. Even though I loved staying with Grandma Henderson in the small hamlet where the Snowy River ran into the sea, loved watching the pelicans glide and hearing the roar the water made when the tide turned, I still found it difficult to be away from home and after a week or so would begin to 'fret', as Grandma called it. So why wouldn't Hanaka fret for her home? No matter how terrible it may have been in the war, it must be awful to know you would never go back. I wanted so much to make her smile.

I suggested we get the hose and water her garden. I found the hose and a sprinkler attachment in the shed. Except for a large tree with lush summery leaves hanging down over the back fence from the next door garden, there was nothing pleasing about the dry and scrappy garden.

'We could fix up your garden,' I said. 'Let's make a Japanese garden!'

Hanaka smiled. 'How is that possible?' she asked.

'You know about Japanese gardens.'

'There are many different kinds of Japanese gardens,' Hanaka said. 'Many, many rules.' She told me that some gardens were only rocks and sand. How could that be any kind of garden?

'I wish I could show you ... Wait. I will draw such a garden for you.' Hanaka said.

She quickly sketched rocks standing among sand raked into long curvy lines. The sand represented rivers or the sea, while the rocks symbolised mountains and islands.

'One must look at this type of garden in a different way, a spiritual way. I think this is hard for a European person,' Hanaka said. It still didn't seem like a garden to me.

More to my taste were the gardens of tea houses which Hanaka described to me, gardens designed to get you into the right frame of mind for the tea ceremony. Hanaka said that it took five years and longer to learn how to perform the tea ceremony. That was a long way from the 'one for each person and one for the pot and make sure the water's boiling' of our household. As well, there were gardens which 'borrowed' the landscape from outside, such as a mountain or a pagoda, to enhance the garden's vista. People flocked to view gardens, Hanaka told me, especially in spring when the cherry blossoms were out and in autumn too when the maples changed colour.

Once, Hanaka's father took her to the famous garden called Kenroku-en near the Sea of Japan in the city of Kanazawa. It was a strolling landscape garden, and its name meant it combined the six attributes necessary to make a perfect landscape garden. She showed me a set of old postcards from her visit to this garden – cherry trees in blossom, wooden bridges over gentle streams and pine trees pruned and shaped in strange ways, the pruning technique called *niwaki*.

'We cannot make a garden, Louise – we do not know the correct rules.'

Why not? I wondered. While it was true that the Japanese garden seemed to have a meaning and purpose for each shrub and tree, rock and hill, leaving nothing to chance or fancy like our English-style gardens, why couldn't we do what we wanted?

27

'Now you're an Australian ... why couldn't we make our own garden to our own rules?' I asked.

All at once Hanaka's face lightened and she laughed.

'Yes! We will make our garden to our own rules!'

However, in order to make a garden, we first needed to learn about gardening, as well as find out if any plants in Australia came from Japan. Walking around Hanaka's garden, she identified a bush with dark-green, polished leaves. The name she gave it was unknown to me, although the bush itself looked familiar. Hanaka tried to explain: 'In winter it has large blooms, white, pink, red. If the rain comes, the blooms are bruised...' It was a camellia! But what if it was the only type of Japanese plant in the whole of Melbourne? And how exactly were Hanaka and I to make her neglected backyard into any kind of Japanese garden – whether by the 'rules' or not? Where would we find rocks, stone lanterns, or moss? How could we possibly build a bridge, or a pond? I needed to find out more, and fast. Oldie was my man.

8

Harry Oldfield, known to my family as Oldie, was our sometime gardener. Although he *was* old, Oldie was strong – a small, wiry man with a weather-beaten face from working outdoors. He drove a battered truck called Pamela, and was always accompanied by his dog, a bitser named Pep – full name Pepe le Moko after a character in some old French film he reckoned he'd seen – and he'd chop back, prune and generally tidy up what my mother never had time to do. After Dad came back from the war, we stopped asking Oldie to come because money was tight, but Dad was too sick to do anything much and after a while Oldie reappeared. He wouldn't take money, but Mum always gave him a hot lunch. My mother loved Oldie – he made her laugh, she said. He called both my mother and me Girlie. 'Hey, Girlie,' he'd shout, 'Give us a loan of ya rippling muscles' or 'What ya think, Girlie? This look pretty enough?'

Our garden was as old as our Victorian-era house, complete with a palm in the front which early each morning and late afternoon became a symphony of bird noises. At the back was a lilly pilly, plus a huge Norfolk Island pine. In their seasons, yellow and pink lilies bloomed and at Christmas, strongly scented white ones, and in their time, early cheer, daffs and johnnies, geraniums, blue hydrangeas, white and pink azaleas. Lily of the valley hid in the shadiest places, and in winter, violets, a favourite pastime of mine being to pick their

9

long delicate stems until I had enough for a small bunch to put in a vase next to my bed so that next morning I awoke to their scent. A Cecile Brunner with its small scented roses grew wildly over a trellis. Even on the hottest day, the garden gave us a shady spot to read or simply to enjoy.

'You bored or something?' Oldie asked. 'Usually I don't see ya for dust.'

I asked Oldie about this plant, that plant. At first he was sceptical.

'What's goin' on?'

'School project,' I told him.

At that, Oldie warmed to his subject. 'A lot of these plants come from the East, ya know, China and that lot. Lilies, China. Chrysanthemums on Mother's Day, also China. Korea, Japan ... Them too.' Oldie pointed to the orange and black-spotted tiger lilies, tall and profuse on one side of the verandah.

'Azaleas. Lots of them over there! Bamboo, different types of it. Beautiful gardens there. Maybe not now ...' Oldie was silent for a moment.

'Terrible business. What else ya want to know, Girlie?'

'That's enough for my project,' I said. 'Thanks Oldie.' I wanted him to go so I could collect a few samples to show Hanaka that afternoon, but Oldie stood there gazing at what seemed to be thin air.

'Terrible business,' he said again, then, 'must be nearly tucker time,' and without further ado, and to my relief, Oldie was gone.

9

Hanaka and I loved to read *The Women's Weekly* and we got into the routine of reading it together on the day it came out each week. Although we read it together for fun, we also read to discover, each for our own reasons, how women were supposed to be. While keeping its readers firmly in the domestic sphere, we were also given a glimpse of worlds far more sophisticated than we could ever aspire to. We read of the latest Paris fashions, 'Dior hides bosom in H look', about visiting theatre and ballet companies, which some of us did get to see, of film stars and Royalty. Royalty, particularly the British, was a constant source of fascination. When the young Queen Elizabeth visited Australia, every outfit, every hat, every handbag was examined by middle-class Australian women, who then attempted to copy them. Her Majesty's hats were especially popular and much cheaper versions of them were sold in the department stores, Buckley and Nunn and Myer. There were advertisements too in *The Weekly*: for perfumes, cleaning products, and remedies for heartburn and constipation as well as more sinister aids to help with the darker moments of a housewife's life, 'Aspro – so kind to the nerves' and 'Relaxa-Tabs' for 'worry, overwork, grief and sleeplessness'.

Hanaka read every bit of *The Weekly*, including these advertisements, often asking me to explain about the various products. She'd been taught English by her father, she'd said.

I knew her father was now dead, and although she rarely mentioned him, I sensed it was because she missed him still. Would I miss my father if he was dead? Whenever this thought came into my head, I wanted to send it hurtling away because it made me feel kind of shaky – with both terror and guilt. I *would* miss him but sometimes when he'd been really bad, even though I knew it wasn't his fault, I wished him, if not quite dead, at least far, far away.

It wasn't until one afternoon when I saw a pile of books on Hanaka's sideboard, including *Gone with the Wind*, that I realised she was, like me, a great reader. I was in for even more surprises.

'You'll love it,' I told Hanaka, referring to the copy of *Gone with the Wind*.

'I have already read this book – in Japanese,' Hanaka said, laughing at my astonished expression. It was a revelation to me and one which forced me to face the fact that there existed another Japan from the Japan of wartime, the Japan my family hated and feared. Hanaka told me of one famous Japanese writer called Junichiro Tanizaki, who had written a book called *The Makioka Sisters*.

'It is about a world now gone, but some people don't want to know that.'

What did she mean? Hanaka answered my silent question.

'My aunt, she is still thinking Japan and its old ways will return, and my cousins wish to marry men they consider their social equal ... but now ... ' But now, what? I wondered.

'The war ... so many men were killed or now are ... not as they were ...'

This was the first time the words 'the war' had been spoken between us. I wanted to read this book, to read about a Japan different from our common knowledge of *Kamikaze* pilots, beheadings and crucifixions of prisoners of war, of brutal domination of Asian populations.

'This book is not in English. I do not think it ever will be.'

I knew why. The war. It had made so many things so very wrong for so many people.

'It *will* be one day, it will!' I replied, even though I couldn't imagine that ever happening.

How wonderful it would be if I could read the great writers of Japan! I do not know why I did not bring with me a few of my favourites – yes, I do know ... I was going to become an Australian woman and that woman would have no need for Japanese books! How foolish of me. To read these Japanese works would be far more than mere pleasure – it would bring me joy. Perhaps in time it may be possible for Chie to send me a few of these books. But I fear Louise is not correct in her belief that one day the world may be able to read an English translation of some of our most famous literature: I fear the world will only ever see my people as people of war.

Father believed that English was the language of modernity – he had studied English at university and then travelled to San Francisco where he worked for a number of years before he married – but as anti-Western sentiment grew in the years preceding the war he asked me, shortly before his death, to destroy our English books and to only ever speak our own language. Heartbroken, I prepared to do as he asked, but could not bring myself to throw to the flames five rare editions which my father and I had read together when I was eleven. In that year, my dearest mother, a wasted child-like figure, finally died. To help pass the long winter nights where, still, one or the other of us would suddenly pause as if alert to a sound that might be a sigh, a breath, a faint call, my father and I read the pride of English literature to each other for comfort as we tried to adjust to a world without my mother. During the war, I never revealed my knowledge of English.

Of the many gifts my father gave to me, his gift of the English language is the one which I have reason to be most grateful for, as to be able to read is now a balm for all the

33

worrying or difficult situations of my new life, a balm that gives me the strength to persevere. Yet ... to read Natsume Soseki's works or Eiji Yoshikawa's great classic, Shin Heike Monogatari! *Then, I could endure all that this new life demands of me.*

10

Summer's blistering heat and northerly winds gave way to the delicious mellow days and cool nights of autumn, but such was the tension in our house, the air seemed unbreathable. My father's condition, which had gradually worsened over the last few months, reached a point where he was unable to get out of bed. Although Mum tried to keep her fears from us, I knew exactly what was happening but acted as if everything was alright for Johnno's sake. Mum wanted my father to go back into hospital.

'No, no,' I heard him plead, 'don't make me go back there, Kitty.'

Too afraid to leave Dad alone, afraid he would harm himself, Mum sat with him all day for a week in their bedroom, except when Maggie relieved her when she returned from her job as a clerk in the railways. My every sense was stretched to its limit, watching, listening, waiting and I had a constant stomach ache. Finally, Aunt Maggie made the decision, taking my weeping father and my distressed mother to hospital. It was a relief to have him gone – a relief with not one shred of joy. My mother came home many hours later and I helped her to bed. Next morning, I got Johnno up and took him to school, leaving Mum to sleep in. She slept until lunchtime, she told me.

As Mum now had to journey every day by bus and train to the Repatriation Hospital, which was a long way from our house, it became my responsibility to look after Johnno when school finished, as well as to shop and start preparing the evening meal. My greatest anxiety was how to keep seeing Hanaka. During the summer holidays when we'd first met, I hadn't needed to tell outright lies in order to see her – I just left out what I didn't want anyone else to know. Now, with my new responsibilities, I had to tell outright lies. I let my friend Libby believe she couldn't come to my place because of my father's illness; that I couldn't come to hers, because my mother needed me. To the woman who picked Johnno up from school, Mrs Webb, I gave a variety of excuses for collecting Johnno past the agreed time: the bus was late; I was kept in; choir practice and a whole lot more. I made sure I was never so late that Mrs Webb tired of it. I took advantage of her kindness because I believed she wouldn't complain to my mother. By telling all these lies, I was able to visit Hanaka for half an hour nearly every afternoon. We sat on the back porch, drinking frosty-cold lemonade while I made her laugh. Afterwards, I ran as hard as I could all the way to Mrs Webb's house; I became very fit, so fit I was soon to qualify for the races in the school sports!

One afternoon, I raced as usual to Hanaka's back door, only to have it opened by a woman with tightly permed hair, a crimson gash of a mouth, and her ample form held firmly in place by a full-body corset commonly called a Berlei, one of the makers of such garments.

'So,' Mother McDonald said, looking me up and down, 'you're the girl who helps Hanaka.' Pearl and gilt earrings sat on the occasional table. Her ear lobes were fat.

'Dear, give me another splash, will you?' Hanaka hesitantly poured more sherry into her mother-in-law's lipstick-smeared glass. Mother McDonald imperiously raised her hand to stop only when the glass was filled to the brim.

'That's far too much!' Her voice was very bossy. Did she think Hanaka was deliberately trying to make her drunk? Mother McDonald took a large mouthful.

'Will we ever make a true Australian housewife out of her?' she laughed – with me, but at Hanaka.

'Little Hanaka quite ruined our Sunday roast by putting cheese sauce all over the vegetables! Can you imagine? Parsley sauce is the only sauce to put on vegetables!'

I thought Mother McDonald was awful, and the worst thing was, I sensed Hanaka was afraid of her.

When I arrived at Hanaka's house a few days later, she greeted me in a very subdued way.

'I am so sorry, but my ... my husband tells me I must ask you if your parents know you come here.'

My heart stopped.

'Of course they know.' Now I was even lying to Hanaka!

'Mother McDonald says that your parents would not like it ...'

The old bitch! Maggie occasionally used that word, much to my mother's horror.

'Your parents please will write a note this is permitted ... for you to come to my house ...'

'I'll bring the letter from my mother tomorrow.' Soon Hanaka was smiling again.

When Mother McDonald asked why Louise was coming to visit me, I did not understand fully what she meant.

'Hasn't she got friends her own age?' she said. 'It's odd. I bet her parents don't know she comes here.' She made 'a fuss' as Alan calls it. Alan does not like it when his mother makes a fuss and so he agrees to many things he doesn't really believe so that she will stop. I wish he would not do this. Alan said I must ask Louise if her parents knew she visited me. Before Louise came into my life, the days were very long because Alan left each morning at 7 o'clock, and all my household duties were finished well before 9 o'clock. At first I wondered if there were other tasks I should be doing, tasks

known only to Australian housewives. I asked Mother McDonald and all she said was that 'a woman should never be idle.'

I like to read but Alan said his mother was not a reader, that she thought reading was a lazy occupation. The way he said this made me know that Alan didn't agree with this view, but he did say that it was best to put my books away when his mother visited me. She does so each week and I am filled with nervousness beforehand. Alan asked me to be patient, that his mother would eventually accept me. I do not think this is so. Always, she talks about a girl called Carol O'Connor. This Carol O'Connor was in love with Alan before the war. Mother McDonald tells me often how beautiful Carol O'Connor is.

Sometimes the lady at number forty-five, Mrs Parker, invites me to afternoon tea. Mrs Parker is quite old and is a Quaker. She explained to me that they have what they call a Meeting and sit silently waiting for what she calls, 'divine leadings'. She tells me not to worry if I don't understand. Mrs Parker often has other ladies at her house and they ask me many questions about how the war was for the people of Japan and about the bombing of Hiroshima and Nagasaki. They mean to be kind but these questions are difficult for me. I remember many things that I do not wish to speak of: a photo in the newspaper of a group of orphans arriving back from Manchuria at the end of the war, one young girl of about ten years carrying the ashes of her dead family in a cloth bag tied around her neck; my terrible shock when details of the mass murders committed by the Japanese Imperial army in Nanjing and Manila were first revealed to the Japanese public during the Tokyo War Crimes trials.

Mrs Parker told me that her prayers are for the world to be at peace. She prays for the people of Japan also. When I told Alan this he laughed in an unhappy way and said, 'She must be the only one.' What did he mean? Would there not be other people in the world who would pray for us Japanese? Even though many bad deeds were committed in our name so, too, did we suffer greatly. Surely Jesus of the Christians would

38

have prayed for us? Tonight, I will silently pray that Louise will bring the letter of permission from her mother. Without Louise my days would be very long.

Taking as my guide the memory of the letters Mum wrote when I stayed at Libby's or other girls' houses, I began, 'Dear Mrs McDonald'. No, it would be better if I wrote to both Hanaka and Alan. I took the letter Mum had started writing to Grandma Henderson, and began copying her handwriting.

12th March,'54

Dear Mr and Mrs McDonald,

I am writing to let you know I am pleased for my daughter, Louise, to visit your home. She tells me she helps Mrs McDonald with her English conversation. I do hope this is useful. Should Louise outstay her welcome, please send her straight home.

Yours sincerely,
Katherine Reid

I was rather pleased with my effort, until I remembered what I was actually doing – forging my mother's signature, deceiving all the people I cared about most in the world. I read what my mother had written to Grandma Henderson.

Sunday

Dear Mum,

Please don't worry about me, I am doing well. Jack is a lot better and the doctors at the Repat are very hopeful, so you see, there's no need for you to come down to Melbourne.

I promise I will let you know if I need you ...

I wasn't the only one in the family telling lies! My mother was telling whoppers! I wanted Grandma Henderson to come but, if she did, I might not be able to see Hanaka. It was all the fault of the war. It had ruined everything. Sudden tears ran down my face, splashing onto my forgery.

11

My father came home from hospital subdued, easier to live with, but, it was plain for us all to see, a man who was only a shadow of how he should have been. Our family life continued much as before, and I distracted myself by juggling things constantly in order to keep my secret life safe, as well as dreaming up various ways in which Hanaka and I could implement our Japanese garden plan. Then, out of the blue, Maggie took herself off in a direction none of us could ever have envisioned. She worked as a clerk in the Victorian Railways, which was heavily unionised, and apparently she went to a union meeting where she met Bill, a union official, and was converted to the cause of the trade union movement – what came first, the conversion or Bill, was a moot point. Bill was a 'charismatic sort of bloke', my father said, quoted Marx and Engels, as well as Yeats, and loved a beer. My mother, a Country Party voter, was a bit horrified by Bill's revolutionary politics, but my father, a Labor man in most instances, was not troubled. As for Maggie, she was well and truly smitten. Bill didn't believe in the sanctity of marriage, so the wife and two children he closeted away somewhere were not revealed to Maggie until she was too far in to want to get out. He told her this family was the result of mistakes he had made when young. We didn't learn about his family for some months and, even then, I only found out because I overheard Mum and Maggie arguing about it.

'He'll never divorce, Maggie. He'll never marry you.'

'That bourgeois bull-dust! I don't need it!' Maggie said.

My eyes were popping out of my head! My Aunt Maggie with a married man who sometimes stayed overnight! In the spare room, which, when I peeked in, didn't look like anything other than a dust mite had slept there! I liked Bill, because he always treated me like a grown-up, and flirted in a courtly kind of way. The other reason I liked him was that he was really respectful toward my father, ready with a beer and a joke, and happy to sit with Dad on the back verandah and yarn over a smoke.

'What do you talk about with Dad?' I asked him once. I found talking to my father very difficult.

'Stickybeak!' Bill pretended shock, then, suddenly serious, he said, 'Your Dad likes to talk about the war ... Not the real stuff – none of us talk about the real stuff – we only talk about the stupid, silly stuff ... The characters we met, the pranks, never the real stuff.' Then he patted me on the shoulder.

'It's hard for the family to understand,' he said, 'which makes it all bloody impossible ...'

Sometimes I heard Maggie and Bill come home on a Saturday night after they'd been out dancing or drinking and discussing politics with like-minded friends. I could hear the deep timbre of Bill's voice and Maggie's intoxicated laugh, then a line or two from a poem or political speech followed by shushing and more laughter as they attempted a quiet entrance into our house. Then, when the house was silent again, I listened very hard, but Maggie's room was too far away from mine to hear anything. Did the earth move for Maggie and Bill? That intoxicated laugh, Bill's voice, deep and sensual, their pleasure at being in each other's company, told me it surely did. Maggie had a new vigour about her, a sort of intense shine. I thought this relationship thrilling. In olden times, Maggie could have been branded with a scarlet letter – A for adultery – just like Hester Prynne, even though it was really Bill who was committing the adultery. Rolling that word

42

around in my mouth, saying it out loud, feeling its sensual lawlessness thrilled me even as I knew that good girls didn't have sex until they were married – that to have sex was to risk all, because if you got pregnant and didn't have a shotgun wedding you might have to give your baby up for adoption.

Mum told me she didn't approve of Maggie and Bill living as husband and wife, even though she liked Bill, but, she said, he was a charmer and one day he'd be off, maybe back to his poor wife. I asked her what would happen if Maggie got pregnant. 'She wouldn't be so silly,' Mum replied. What did she mean? 'There are ways,' Mum said, but even when I pressed her with 'How?' she would only say that when I was going to be married, a doctor would tell me. But Maggie wasn't married and she knew – it wasn't fair that I didn't! This sort of talk clearly embarrassed Mum whose only advice to date on such matters was 'to never let a man put his hands down there'. Mum told me to tell anyone who might be rude enough to ask that Maggie and Bill were married – to tell these nosy Parkers that Bill had lost his wife (he had indeed) and he and Maggie had met and married very quickly 'In ... in ... say, Newcastle,' Mum said.

Aunt Maggie was now moving in a world both earthier and more sophisticated than ours. I gained new respect for her, even though she now delivered lectures to us on the working class, Marx, Lenin and the Revolution if we weren't quick enough to avoid her. Although I couldn't imagine such a thing as a revolution happening here in Melbourne, I was willing for Maggie to believe what she liked, because she was less embittered and more generous in her dealings with me and Johnno. Maggie was happy, and this was the first time I would ever have called her that.

12

I'd long wanted to see Hanaka wearing a *kimono*, but whenever I'd asked, she always laughingly said she was a modern woman and now an Australian housewife. I'd forget about *kimonos* for a while, only to remember again, but I was careful not to plague her. One day I was rewarded for my patience.

'Your *kimono* is so beautiful,' I said, as soulfully as I could, indicating a photo of Hanaka and Alan on their wedding day. I sighed in a way I hoped would melt her heart. 'Come,' she said, leading me to the bedroom – a room whose door was always shut. From a large wooden chest, its lock decorated with a bird, Hanaka took out a parcel and carefully unwrapped it to reveal a *kimono* of the softest gradations of pink to mauve with flowers woven into the fabric and embroidered with birds – cranes, Hanaka told me – using silver, gold and a dark purple thread. The *kimono* was far more exquisite than the photo showed. 'See how the cranes are flying?' Hanaka said. 'This means many good wishes.' Hanaka then took out a long sash, the colour of the sea on a cloudy day.

'This is called an *obi*,' she explained, 'and is tied around the *kimono*, like you see in the wedding photo.' The *obi* was so long it surely could be wrapped around several women, and was lavishly embroidered with flowers in deep to the palest of pinks, as well as leaves, with occasional white and silver embroidery on both flowers and leaves to indicate snow. Hanaka said to me in a playful way, 'You should recognise this flower, Louise.' The flower did look familiar. What was it?

'Camellia!' Hanaka said. 'Alan chose this design,' she added.

Completely enchanted by the *kimono* and *obi*, I barely noticed what Hanaka said about Alan, nor that she had taken another parcel from the chest. But when I caught a glimpse of white and red silk, I was all attention. Hanaka spread out on the bed a *kimono* of white silk, exquisitely embroidered with white flowers accentuated by silver and soft pink, and lined with scarlet silk. It took my breath away.

'It was my mother's wedding *kimono*,' Hanaka said.

'Why didn't you wear it at your own wedding?' I asked.

'This *kimono* is for a Shinto marriage ceremony. Because I was married in a Christian ceremony, it was not proper to wear it.'

Hanaka showed me an old photo of her mother and father on their wedding day. The photo showed a formal looking young couple: the woman in the white *kimono*, her hair elaborately dressed with ornate pins and the man in a dark *kimono*. The man and woman looked like actors out of an old-fashioned film, yet they were Hanaka's parents, just as Kitty and Jack were mine. It hardly seemed credible. Perhaps looking at these treasures made Hanaka sad, because she began to wrap up the *kimonos* and I didn't press her to put on her wedding *kimono*. Hanaka's treasures were, I understood, all that she had left of her life in Japan.

It was a joy to me to be able to speak to Louise of the happy memories I had of girlhood outings to tea houses and gardens, to view the cherry blossoms or catch fire-flies. Louise was eager to learn about my life in Japan but I only spoke of happy things, only the events suitable for such a girl to hear. I never

spoke of the suffering and sadness – Louise would know nothing of what had happened, how after the Emperor told us we must 'embrace defeat' and 'endure the unendurable', for most Japanese life was almost as hard, except that now there were no more bombs. How hundreds of thousands of homeless people throughout the country sheltered in railway stations. That these people, orphans, war widows, returned soldiers, even survivors of the bombs of Hiroshima and Nagasaki were deemed by Japanese society to no longer belong to a proper social category because they were homeless. I had been influenced by my father's interest in Western democracy; he had often pondered whether we Japanese could ever really embrace democracy with its beliefs in the equality of all peoples. He sometimes read out sections from a book written in the 1700s by an American, Thomas Paine, called Rights of Man. Father believed our centuries of isolation had kept us backwards politically. Few would have agreed with him. Perhaps that is why he spoke only to me about these matters and I witnessed myself the terrible prophecy of his words.

We were all hungry in those years: rice was unobtainable except on the blackmarket and heirlooms, in families for generations, were exchanged for a paltry amount of it. The Occupation Forces had left the Japanese to sort out our own affairs and it took many years before rice became available and affordable to ordinary people. In the meantime, we were told by the Authorities to add grasshoppers and acorns to our diet. Respectable people died slowly of starvation, sometimes doing so in order for members of their families to survive. It was a time I would like to forget.

13

Johnno and I were waiting for Mum to come back from work and then we were going into town to see *Knights of the Round Table* starring Robert Taylor and Ava Gardner with some money Grandma Henderson sent us. A few weeks before, Mum had started working part-time at the local newsagent because the government still wouldn't give Dad a full pension and money was very tight. We had to wait for Mum as she always insisted on inspecting us, as well as warning us against speaking to strange men. When he was younger, this would puzzle Johnno: 'What would happen?' he asked me once, 'If I said "Ho, ho, jelly bean" to a strange man?' I said the strange man would think we were loons and run away. For quite some time afterwards, whenever a lone man glanced our way, Johnno would whisper his magic spell, 'Ho, ho, jelly bean.'

My father sat on the back verandah smoking his pipe and, although seeming to gaze out at the garden, he was largely in his own private place. Johnno was making a model plane and I was reading.

'Dad, where does this bit go?' Johnno asked. Dad broke free from his thoughts and looked at the balsawood model and then the instructions.

'Look, Johnno. See? Glue it here.'

'Dad, you've been on a plane, haven't you?'

'Yeah, a lot of planes,' Dad replied.

'But you weren't a pilot?'

47

'No ... I was a foot soldier ... on the ground ...'

'Where'd you sleep?'

'Any place I could ... sometimes I didn't ... too dangerous ...'

'What did you eat? Did you have to eat grubs?'

'Have you cleaned your teeth?' I broke in. 'I bet you haven't, go on and do it now. Mum'll be home in a minute.' Not true, but I wanted to break up his questioning Dad because sometimes it made Dad start obsessing and we never knew where that would end up. Poor Johnno was forever trying to find clues about our father – once I'd caught him looking in Dad's chest of drawers and I knew he was searching for something I'd long given up on. If only Dad could get a job, one that he could do without any stress, then he wouldn't sit at home all day, thinking, thinking, always about the awful war.

Oldie came around the back of the house pushing a wheelbarrow with his shovel and other gardening equipment in it, as well as some seedlings.

'G'day, Jack.' Oldie shook Dad's hand. 'I was hoping to find ya here,' Oldie said.

As if my father wasn't almost always here.

'Need ya help with these.' Oldie pointed to the seedlings.

'Me! I'll help!' Johnno forgot all about the plane he was making.

'Little mate, it's ya Dad's help I need today,' Oldie said, 'but come and watch and see what he does...'

Oldie gave me a kind of glance that conveyed he knew what he was doing. Oldie had known my father since Dad was a boy living in our house with his mother and father. Apparently, Dad used to have an enviable vegetable garden, combined with carnations and dahlias. I've forgotten which, flowers or vegetables, but he'd won several prizes at the Royal Melbourne Show.

'What's Oldie up to?' I asked Mum when she came home. 'He's helping Dad with the garden.' Mum was pleased.

48

'What a kind man Oldie is,' she said. 'Holding out a hand to your father the best way he knows – gardening. Maybe, by reminding Dad of the pleasure of growing things, he's hoping to get Dad more interested in the ...' Mum looked so sad, I wished I'd said nothing. She took a deep breath.

'More interested in the future ...' Her expression suggested that she didn't like Oldie's chances much, but both of us were moved by Oldie's attempt.

Before Johnno and I left for town, Mum tried to persuade me to wear a stupid little yellow hat, but I baulked at it. I did wear white mesh gloves and my black court shoes with bows, and was allowed to put on some pale-pink lipstick. I was supposed to be a 'young lady' and a lady always wore a hat and gloves when she went to town for lunch and a show or to a Red Cross or some other 'do'. These 'rules' were a bit like the rules the characters in Jane Austen's novels had to follow if they wanted to be thought of as repectable. But that had been more than a century ago!

How I wished I was Ava Gardner! Or even the girl who worked in the local solicitor's office who wore shocking-pink lipstick and smart little suits with high heels and an air of doing exactly as she pleased! I wanted to leave school as soon as I turned fifteen, but Mum was dead against it. She wanted me to train in something. She thought me clever enough to maybe even become a teacher.

'I wish I'd been trained to be a stenographer or a nurse,' Mum had said, 'something that would give me a good wage, but we were all brought up to believe that when we married, our husband would support us. Don't ever rely on that, Louise. You never know if you'll have to support a family one day and a training could be the difference between managing or not.'

She was talking about herself, but what had happened to my mother was never going to happen to me! I *would* wear high heels and shocking-pink lipstick, and be free to do precisely as I liked.

While Johnno and I were buying lollies to eat in the pictures, I saw that boy from my school, Toluk, with two younger children, both blond like him, who I figured were his sister and brother. Fortunately, Toluk had given up his leather shorts for khaki Aussie ones, so I didn't need to feel embarrassed for him anymore, yet my face still burned. Toluk looked at me, then away; I looked in his direction, then away; finally we both looked at the same time. Toluk smiled. My heart did a small flip as I smiled back and gave him a slightly queenly wave.

Toluk sat some way behind Johnno and me because Johnno liked to sit up the front of the theatre; it made him feel like he was in it, he said. All through the film, I was aware that Toluk could be looking at me, which rather distracted me from looking at Ava. The moment the film finished, I stood up so as not to miss him before he left. Toluk was still there, and he waved.

When Johnno and I got home, I pulled out the atlas in order to see exactly where the Ukraine, as I'd learned it was called, was. Mum helped me.

'It's here – it's part of the USSR but was occupied by Germany during the war,' Mum said. 'When the war ended a lot of people who didn't want to be under Soviet rule ended up in displaced persons camps and then came to Australia.'

Aunt Maggie happened to be home, and stopped on her way to the kitchen. 'We shouldn't have let them come,' she said. 'They're all bloody Nazis.'
Mum gave me one of her 'don't take any notice of Maggie' looks.

Poor Toluk! To have to leave his country and come to a place where he could hardly speak one word of English. When he first came to school, the mean boys teased him by teaching him all the rudest words, words that nobody ever uttered in public. Toluk eventually twigged, and one afternoon he took on his three main tormentors and beat them all up. After that, Toluk was something of a hero, even more so when he proved a huge asset to the school football team. Toluk was so handsome. He was so brave. Oh, boy! I was in love!

14

'Do some Australian women work after they are married?' Hanaka asked.

'Not usually.' I didn't tell her that my mother now worked because we needed the money she made.

'If you're a doctor or something, you can.'

'I would like, but my husband say women who are married don't work because it is bad for the man's pride, that people would say the man cannot support his wife. It is like this in Japan too, before the war.'

Hanaka went on to say that she would like to work as she had done after the war. She'd worked as a clerk then later as a translator with the Occupation Forces. It seemed so strange to me that people who had been at war with one another, afterwards, worked together. I imagined many humiliations for Hanaka.

'Did you like it?'

'It was most interesting,' Hanaka said. 'Sometimes, very sad, but always interesting. I was paid a little more than my job before, and also was given a free meal. Before, we sometimes had not enough to eat.'

My mouth nearly fell open! Hanaka hungry? I knew soldiers in the war had been hungry, and lots of people almost starving, and even afterwards in Britain there was still rationing because Libby's mother sent food parcels to relatives who lived in Scotland, but what that really meant only hit home when Hanaka said she'd been hungry.

'Our government told us to eat grasshoppers,' Hanaka said. My response to this was such horrified incredulity that she laughed.

'A grasshopper is quite tasty,' she said, her beautiful hand over her laughing mouth.

I would have found it difficult to explain my reaction to Hanaka's hunger – I had read many a historical novel where people were forced to eat all manner of awful things, even rats, but that was fiction which, although I sensed fiction often told more truths than so-called 'fact' books, was still largely about the lives of imaginary people. What hit me now was that I knew someone dear to me, other than my father, who had endured hunger. I remembered Maggie saying during one of her rants about Japanese war brides, that they only married Australian men so they could get a square meal. Remembering this, I hated Maggie with a passion.

During the war and for some years afterwards, I lived with my aunt and two cousins in a small town near Kure. When we heard the Emperor's voice – for the first time ever – telling the people of Japan that we must embrace defeat, Aunt's shock was profound, and even after two years, she had great difficulty in understanding that the way of life she believed in no longer existed. Both her daughters, my cousins, cast in the same mould as their mother and afraid of getting too old to make a correct marriage, wanted marriage negotiations to be started. But who were they to marry? So many men dead on foreign ground, so many boxes containing their ashes waiting for collection throughout the country. The men who did return alive were shunned, even by their own families, who were shamed that the soldier had chosen surrender rather than death – every soldier had been issued a hand grenade to ensure he would end his own life rather than be captured.

53

My aunt and cousins were ill-equipped to survive this time of great hardship and it was my duty to help them, but my meagre salary as an accounts clerk was not enough to buy the food we needed. My cousins believed our old family name kept them from doing menial jobs, and as they had no other skills neither of them worked. They spent the day fretting about being unmarried and being hungry.

After more than two months passed in which we ate no rice, Aunt called me to her room where her wooden chest stood open. Only the day before, the Asahi newspaper had reported the death from starvation of a respected scholar at the University. Although Aunt had sold many items of value, she still possessed kimonos, antique kanzashi – hairpins – tortoise-shell combs, fans and other heirlooms. She picked up a parcel which she undid and showed me a kimono of the finest silk, surely dating back to late Edo and proudly worn by one of our ancestors. With great dignity, Aunt handed me the kimono. I imagined a sly merchant fingering the silk as if it was a coarse rag, then offering me an insulting price after which he would carelessly throw the kimono into an overflowing basket. I bowed low. 'Honourable Aunt. This belongs to my cousins.'

I had already sold most of my own possessions. All that were left were my father's books and my mother's wedding kimono. These precious possessions had for me a great spiritual value, and each morning I visited the temple near Aunt's home to pray to Kannon, the Goddess of Mercy. I prayed for her help so that I would never have to sell these last links to my mother and my father. That afternoon, I prayed most fervently for the Goddess to grant me the wisdom to know what to do. I asked for her to give me the courage to sell the wedding kimono and the rare books if I must.

On the way home from work I chanced upon a conversation between two women who worked as cleaners in the soldiers' quarters of the British Commonwealth Occupation Forces who I knew to be Australian. The women were recalling the story of one soldier's silly prank on another, and the way they spoke of these men was as if they were favourite naughty boys. It was then that I realised the Goddess had answered my entreaties: I would seek a position with the Occupiers as a translator. Such a position would be better paid and enable us all to have more to eat. I pledged again never to sell my precious keepsakes and I have kept my pledge.

To carry out my plan to become a translator with the Occupation Forces took all of my courage. Firstly, I had to overcome my fear of the Australian soldiers who I'd heard hated Japanese men because of the bitter battles fought in the Pacific, but who liked our women very much.

More difficult to overcome was Aunt's objections. Despite becoming quite frail because of our poor diet, she was opposed to me taking this position. 'It will go against our name. It will lessen the chances of your cousins to marry into good families. Your father would never have allowed it.' Aunt did not say these words directly, this is not the Japanese way, rather, her various comments were delivered with great subtlety and restraint.

Aunt's views were very different from those of her brother, my father. I did not tell her of his anguish when Japan occupied Manchuria, of his involvement in a group opposed to Japanese militarism. Nor that the reason he committed suicide – that Japan's military expansion had so depleted our country's resources making it impossible for his illness to be treated properly – was coupled with despair at the war he saw coming and of his fears for me if I had to stay and nurse him.

Finally I did something that would never have happened before the war: I made the decision to get this job my own. Unless I acted, I feared we would all slowly starve.

At the railway station on my way to the interview in Kure, I carefully stepped around puddles from the recent rain, wanting to protect my better kimono, blue with a spray of autumn grass. I saw a boy of about nine who I had seen several times before. This boy always held the stub of a cigarette between his teeth, and kept his oversized shorts held up by a piece of rope and today used a bag which might once have held charcoal, to keep warm. I dropped a parcel

55

containing three balls made of a mixture of bread, potato and soybean waste into the boy's filthy hand. 'Tasukete kurete arigatoo (Thank you for helping me,)' he said as he bowed. A corpse lay in the far corner, waiting to be collected. Someone had placed a scrap of cloth over the face.

The translation test I was given was quite easy and, although my words felt awkward during the conversation section, the officer who interviewed me seemed pleased. He told me I had the position but must first undergo a medical examination which, although embarrassing, I passed.

'I would like to do something more than care for the home,' Hanaka said.

'And the garden,' I reminded her.

Hanaka said she would like to learn how to paint using watercolour. In art at school we'd learnt about the great painters like Leonardo da Vinci and Michelangelo and we'd done a bit about the painters who used to work around the Heidelberg area on the outskirts of Melbourne which was still very bushy. Our art teacher had shown us a picture of one of these paintings called *Moonrise: Heidelberg* by an artist called Emanuel Phillips Fox.

'We could go to the Art Gallery,' I suggested. 'During my next school holidays.' I'd been only once, ages ago, because whenever we went somewhere special, we always chose the zoo or the aquarium.

'There might be an artist living around here who would give you lessons.'

I had never before considered such a possibility, but as my own art teacher at school was an artist, maybe there were others like him. I could ask my teacher, but I didn't say that to Hanaka in case I lost my nerve about doing it.

'I don't think my husband ...'

Although he looked dashing in the photos around the house, I'd been so careful to avoid bumping into Alan, I'd never actually met him. Their meeting and marriage certainly was romantic but this didn't protect him from my judgement that the reality of the transition from romantic lover to husband was a great disappointment. Also he was the son of the awful interfering Mother McDonald – couldn't he see that his mother was unkind to Hanaka? Learning now that Hanaka was concerned that Alan could put a dampener on her wish to paint, he sank further in my estimation. Was he so selfish that he feared if Hanaka learned to paint, she wouldn't be able to cook his tea on time?

My idea of being grown up was that you no longer needed to ask permission to do what you wanted, but being a wife and mother seemed to stop a woman doing anything but cook and clean. Maybe it would be better not to be married at all but to be like … like … I tried scouring my memory for a suitable model from literature … but all I could find were women who were punished for disregarding convention or who were eccentric, but poor, old aunts, or headmistresses or even nuns. In the film *Gentlemen Prefer Blondes* Marilyn and Jane wanted to gather as many diamonds as possible and to marry a terribly old but rich husband. Marilyn and Jane needed all the diamonds because rich men were particularly feckless and when they lost their looks these rich old husbands were sure to abandon them. Unless of course the old husbands died before the looks went, in which case Marilyn and Jane would inherit a fortune. Even through the film's seductive glamour, I thought Marilyn and Jane inferior sort of heroines because all they seemed to care about was money, until they fell in love, in which case they cared not a hoot about it any more. Also, they never read books. So I was left with the nuns, et cetera, as the standard for the unmarried state, or Maggie, who at least had sex, and was the best model I could find in real life, but I was pretty sure she'd marry Bill in a flash if he were free.

'Ask Alan. Tell him how happy you'd be.'

'I do not think …'

'Australian husbands need to be told something a few times before they understand what you want.' I'd said this off

57

the top of my head, but maybe it was true. Women, I'd long observed, seemed to have to tell men many times to fix something, or fetch something, before the task actually got done.

'Try it. No harm in trying, is there?'

No harm either, in trying to get something happening with our Japanese garden, but I wasn't very hopeful, and I was right. Alan was too busy and needed to relax when he wasn't working, Hanaka said.

How I wished I could do the digging, but I'd already tried and the ground was rock hard. Now, it seemed, our garden must wait until Alan was able. Romantic hero indeed! Husbands were another kettle of fish altogether!

I never imagined myself being a woman having a love relationship with a foreign soldier whose country did not want her, and at first refused her permission to enter as his wife. I never imagined ever leaving my homeland. I became such a woman one bitterly cold January day when the rain and the wind joined together and swept everything in its path, including myself.

I was on an errand when this double force knocked me off my feet and I was helped up by the officer who was to become my husband. He introduced himself as Alan McDonald and, after taking me to shelter, asked if he could meet me the next evening so we could talk. He asked me to name a place where I would be at ease but I only knew of makeshift stalls because food was so scarce and expensive. He said he could take me to a place he knew but that other servicemen would be there. I was anxious because the Australians were forbidden to fraternise with Japanese women. Many of these women were prostitutes and could be picked up at any time by the military police and subjected to examinations for venereal disease because the Australian authorities were alarmed about the high incidence of these

58

diseases amongst the troops. This had happened to some women who were not prostitutes, but had formed love relationships with Australian servicemen.

'It's not fair,' Alan said. 'The Yanks are allowed to have Japanese girlfriends, but not us.' Alan told me he would look after me.

I was, by this time, twenty-two years, still young enough by Japanese standards to find a husband but I had not been alone in the company of a man for many years. I was inexperienced in love. When I was much younger, I liked my friend Chie's brother very much, but he went to war and died fighting in the Burma campaign. Now, unlike my cousins, I held no illusions as to the chances of my marrying and I would only marry for love. At the time I met Alan, I wanted to forget the past and, unable to imagine the future, I lived only in the present.

At the restaurant, Alan smiled and smiled as I kept on eating. I can remember, still, how delicious everything tasted! He kept re-ordering more of my favourite dishes. Later he told me he'd never seen such a small girl eat so much with such delicacy! As I ate, Alan told me about the battles in Syria and Palestine in which he had fought, about his home in Melbourne and his longing to return to civilian life. The next time we met, he spoke of long holidays playing cricket on the beach with his brother and cousins, and afterwards, sitting on the sand watching the waves and the sun set while eating cold roast meat sandwiches for 'tea'. 'When I was hungry, plagued by the heat, eaten alive by insects and just plain terrified, remembering those times helped get me through,' he said.

Alan told me too that he wanted a peaceful life and marrying a Japanese woman would not give him that. I said I would never leave Japan. A woman I worked with had warned me that some foreign servicemen promised marriage but then went back to their country leaving the woman, sometimes with a child. Such a child would never be accepted into Japanese society. I had heard that some people referred to these children in disgust as ainoko – mongrels. I was as confused

59

as to what I wanted from Alan as he was regarding me. We agreed it would be best for us not to meet again.

15

Hanaka had to go away to the country to meet more McDonald relatives during the next school holidays, which really messed up our gardening plans. She seemed strangely subdued about the impending trip, and something told me it wasn't all down to disappointment in missing out on the gardening.

'Don't you like the people you'll be staying with?' I asked.

'They are my husband's family.' Even though, as we got to know each other, my way of speaking often amused her, Hanaka was sometimes, still, slightly shocked by such direct questions.

'You don't have to like them just because of that. I don't like my Aunt Maggie much, and she doesn't like me.'

'You must not say that, Louise.'

I pressed my advantage. 'Who ...?'

'My husband's brother's wife ... I do not like to be in her house for one week ...'

With Hanaka away, I fell back on my old stand-bys, Johnno and my friend Libby, but Libby was annoyed with me for never being available, and she'd made a new friend. She still wanted to be friends, she said, but we were no longer 'best' friends. I went to her place a couple of times in the first days of the holidays, but her friend Joan proved expert at doing those small things that girls can do so well to make one feel unwanted. Finally, I told Libby I'd come and see her, but only when Joan wasn't there. 'Joan likes to come every day.' Libby was not going to forgive me easily.

Then Mum announced she was going to work full-time at the newsagent's during the rest of the holidays which meant I was going to be responsible for Johnno, as Dad wasn't much good at looking after him. I felt trapped. Wasn't this supposed to be the best time of my life? A time when I was a 'teenager', a concept just gaining acceptance, listening to popular songs on the radio and having mad crushes on singers, movie stars and ordinary boys? It wasn't fair! I said so to Mum, but instead of telling me to stop being a brat, she apologised. Things were very tight, she said, and we needed the extra money she'd make. Did I think she wanted to get up at 5am to lug newspapers and magazines and then work until late afternoon? But she had to, just as I had to help keep the household together. I felt awful, and said I was sorry. She hugged me tightly. Her expression was intensely serious. 'Without your help, Lou,' Mum said, 'I couldn't do this.' Words were important to me. I read attentively, and I listened the same way. That was how I'd gotten closer to Hanaka – by listening and taking cues. When my mother said, 'Without your help … I couldn't do this' did she mean without my help she couldn't do the newsagent's job, or did she mean something far darker? That without my help she couldn't look after us? Without me, she would fall apart and become useless? Her words were just an expression, I tried reasoning, she was in charge of the situation, even if that situation was not entirely to her liking. But I knew my mother very often found her situation difficult to cope with, knew she was not as strong as some other mothers, so if she said such things to me, she must really need my help to keep her end up. My stomach churned.

In my heart I feared we were a family that could fall, held together only by my mother and, behind her, Grandma Henderson, and by Maggie too – at least I didn't think she'd let us starve! But what I wanted most of all was to be rid of this knowledge. I wanted a strong family where we were all safe.

Yes, what I really wanted was a father to look after us. A father unlike the father I had.

Hanaka was supposed to return a few days before my holidays ended, but I didn't know whether her husband would go straight back to work. As I was longing to see her, I decided to walk past her house to see if Alan's Holden was in the driveway or not and, if not, I'd ring the bell in the hope she'd be there. But first I had to get away from home, which proved quite difficult. Then on the second last day of the holidays, Mum came home from work early. She said she had a slight stomach upset and had been sent home. I made her a cup of tea and took it into her bedroom where she was lying fully clothed with her eyes shut. She was perfectly alright, she told me, her stomach would soon settle down. I refused to see how pale, how tired, she looked. I told her Libby had invited me over to her house, my need to see Hanaka being greater than my need to be a dutiful daughter, but the small lie still sat uneasily.

Thankfully, Hanaka was home and I hugged her exuberantly, causing her to step back, slightly alarmed by my embrace.

'Sorry,' we both said at once, then laughed.

'I am not yet used to this Western custom,' Hanaka explained.

'Hugging?'

'In Japan, we do not hug or kiss ... only ... between people in private ... like a man and a woman ...'

'Does Mother McDonald hug you?' I asked.

'She always wants me to kiss her,' Hanaka pointed to her cheek, 'here.'

'And you don't like!' We laughed and laughed.

'What about your holiday?' I asked. Hanaka looked away without speaking, but not before I saw her press her hand to her eyes to stop the tears. What had Alan's awful relatives done to Hanaka?

'Never mind,' I said, 'You're home now.'

63

❖

Alan warned me that his brother's wife, Mary, would not be making polite conversation with me during our visit to them in the country. This was because Mary's brother had been killed by Japanese troops in New Guinea. I asked Alan if I should stay at home.

'You're my wife, Hanaka,' he said. 'I'm entitled to take you to visit my only brother. Mary will have to come to heel on this one. It's been years now and you didn't kill her brother, whatever she might think.'

But when we arrived, I quickly knew that Mary would not be 'coming to heel', a phrase that completely mystified me. When we were introduced, she turned her head away and her five-year-old daughter burst into tears. During the next two days, I tried to make myself very small and quiet, so as not to make the disharmony even more unpleasant, but still the woman's hatred almost sparked off her. Whenever I entered a room Mary left it, and when I offered to help, as I knew was expected of a woman guest, she rudely ignored me. For a woman to behave like this in Japan would be a disgrace to her husband and family. In fact, they would think the woman had gone mad. The little girl could not help staring at me, and although I wanted to make friends with her, I did not, because it would only anger her mother further.

During the evening meal, we spoke little, but then Mary began to talk of this dead brother, how young and handsome he had been, his sense of humour, his devotion to his family. It was as if she could not think, or speak, of anything else, her only desire to go over and over these tragic events.

'Give it a rest, love,' Charlie gently said. Mary did not take any notice of her husband's warning.

'At least he was killed in action,' Mary started. 'Not like the poor bastard they captured. Tied him to a tree and used him as bayonet practice. His mates could hear him screaming and couldn't do anything ... Bloody murderers.'

64

I very much wished not to hear these terrible things.

'Come now, Mary' Alan said. 'If you take away those actions, the Japanese fought with enormous courage.'

Why did my husband say this? It was like 'a red rag to a bull' – a saying I understood perfectly. Perhaps he was defending the Japanese soldiers because of me.

'They were sub-human savages!'

'It's rumoured that after a while neither side took prisoners. Yeah, I know, Mary, it's not the same as using a man for bayonet practice ... but I've talked to blokes who were there... One mate of mine said, "We found one Jap but he was fly-blown, so we took him out and shot him." '

I wished myself far, far away.

'The men who served there hated the Japs' guts with reason! I wouldn't expect you to understand that!'

'But even with the hating, some had a grudging respect for them ... they were a formidable enemy...' Alan countered.

'What would you know? You weren't bloody well there ... and look what you brought home!' Mary stormed out. Then Charlie left the room and we heard arguing in the bedroom.

'I can't stand it! I don't want her in this house!' Mary shouted. Then, a door slammed and Mary, sobbing, ran out into the darkness.

Charlie came out of the bedroom and apologised to Alan. To me he said, 'I'm so sorry, lass. She's never got over it. She adored him and he was only eighteen. Right at the end of it, too.'

Alan said it had been a mistake to have come and we would leave first thing in the morning. He held me tightly, and said, 'Sorry, love. She's unhinged by grief.'

Unable to sleep, I thought of the day a soldier came to my friend Chie's parents' house. The soldier was ragged and thin and hungry, and was on his way to his own home town, not knowing what he would find there. He came to Chie's family home because he and Chie's brother had each pledged that, if one was killed, the other would cut a finger from the body so it could be cremated and the ashes brought back to

65

Japan. This is what the stranger brought Chie and her family: the ash and bone from her brother's severed finger.

That night, despite Alan's arms around me, I could not help the tears that fell. I determined to become like my Quaker neighbour and pray every day for peace in the world.

16

As soon as I saw the way the front fly-wire screen door hung open, I sensed something was wrong.

'Where the hell have you been?' said Maggie as I came through the door. 'We've been looking for you. Where were you?'

Johnno was sitting in the kitchen, red-eyed.

'Mum ... The ambulance came ...' He started to cry.

'Tell me what's happened,' I shouted at Maggie.

'Don't you raise your voice to me,' Maggie shouted back. 'You're never here when you're needed! I sent Johnno around to your friend Libby's, and her mother said you hadn't been there. You're a sly one ... I bet you were with a boy!'

'Tell me!' I screamed. Johnno cried louder.

'She's vomiting blood,' Maggie said. 'All those bloody Aspros she takes.'

I was stunned. We always had a bottle of Aspro at home and I was aware that both my mother and father used them. '*The quick answer to those nervy, headachy spells that come to nearly every housewife is two Aspro tablets with a cup of tea.*' Thus ran the countless advertisements in magazines and newspapers adding that, '*Aspro tablets do not harm the heart or stomach.*' Mum was often nervy and headachy, but she never went to the doctor unless she was really sick. Now, because she'd taken pills which were supposed to make her feel better, she'd made herself sicker.

'Jack insisted he go to hospital with her, which is probably a bad idea, so I'm going there now to sort things out.' Perhaps taking pity on our stricken faces, Maggie said, 'Your mother will be alright. Just needs some blood and time to heal her stomach.' But not too much pity, especially for me.

'As for you, you little hussy, don't you realise this family's got enough problems without you going boy-mad and worrying your mother to death!'

Hussy! Who was the hussy? It certainly wasn't me.

Two days later, Johnno and I stood outside the ward waiting to see our mother. Johnno was fretting terribly for her, his wheezing way worse than it had been for some time. I was so sorry for him, even sorrier than I was for myself, which was very sorry indeed. I was feeling guilty and, worse still, I was going to keep on feeling guilty because I was going to tell Mum not that I was at Hanaka's when I was supposed to be at Libby's, but that I had been meeting a boy. Maggie had tackled me about it the night before but I told her that she, Maggie, was not my mother (thank God, but I didn't say that), and the only person I was going to speak about it to was my mother.

'I'll be keeping a close eye on you,' Maggie said.

A nurse opened the doors of the ward, signalling the start of visiting hour. We walked into a long room which contained perhaps twelve beds down each side. Johnno held my hand tight, and I was as glad of his hand as he was of mine. Dad told us Mum was toward the end of the ward, but we still looked closely at the person in each bed as we passed, fearful we would miss her. Then, a sob bursting from his throat, Johnno rushed to our mother and she enfolded him in her arms. She looked so small in the huge old ward that I suddenly felt I was about to cry too.

The doctors told my mother she had a bleeding peptic ulcer, for which she needed a blood transfusion and then a special diet to allow the ulcer to heal. She had been taking up to twelve Aspro a day, but now she was forbidden to ever take them again. They recommended a quiet life.

'Everything's in white sauce,' Mum told us.

'Even sweets?' Johnno asked.

'Duffer,' Mum tousled his hair.

It was so good to see her. We'd brought her a posy from bits and pieces in the garden. She buried her nose in it.

'Home,' she said.

'When ...?' I wanted her back home *now*.

'When my blood's right and I don't have any more pain.'

Pain? She had pain?

'Lou ...?'

'Mmm?'

'No more lies, darling. Lies always get us into trouble. Promise me?'

'I promise ...'

'Good girl ... I ...'

We were interrupted by the same nurse who had opened the ward doors, now pushing a tea trolley.

'Tea, Mrs Reid? Oops! No tea for you! Some nice warm milk instead.'

'I would love a nice strong cup of tea, but...'

'Your stomach wouldn't!' The nurse looked quickly around and then said to Johnno, 'Like a biscuit?'

She handed Johnno two milk arrowroots, and then did the same to me.

'Don't let Sister see or I'll be in big trouble.'

When the nurse had moved on to the next patient, Mum said, 'She's only been on the wards for three weeks. Poor girl's always getting into trouble about something. When I was admitted, she told me not to be frightened, that I'd get used to it like she'd done. I do admire her ... always so kind and cheerful.'

I longed for my mother to admire me too, but because of my lies, she never could.

My mother was to stay in hospital for two weeks. Because of school, and Maggie's union commitments, we could only visit her on the weekends. Dad's one visit when Mum was admitted had left him nervy and tearful, so Maggie told him he mustn't go again. Maggie could be very firm, even hard, on her brother, but he took more notice of what she said than he did of Mum. With Mum in hospital, Dad settled down to a diet of beer and brandy. As he was relatively well-behaved, despite his drinking, I guess Maggie simply didn't have the will to deal with it. I wasn't much of a cook but I was better than Maggie, and for that first week we made do with makeshift meals, mainly sausages and bread, which Johnno loved, and on a couple of nights Bill cooked, once a delicious shepherd's pie and another time a leg of lamb that had 'fallen off the back of a truck', he said, which left Johnno puzzling. Bill was there most nights, sometimes not arriving until very late when we were all in bed. One night he arrived with another leg of lamb and a bottle of Yardley English Lavender perfume for Maggie, and a book for me. 'Sorry,' he said to Johnno, 'but the back of the truck didn't run to a present for you. Another time, matie.' The book was called *Caddie* and was the real-life story of a Sydney barmaid during the Great Depression. Maggie laughed when she saw it.

'You'll make a Socialist of her yet, Bill, and Kitty won't like that!'

One night, in the middle of the week, I awoke in a fright convinced something bad had happened to Mum. We didn't have the telephone, though Maggie said we were getting it on very soon, so if we needed to phone we went into Mrs Box's place. It was after midnight when I woke, too late to ring, and anyhow, Mum would think something terrible had happened at home, that is, if something terrible hadn't happened to her. Not to mention Mrs Box herself, who really would think the Lord had finally come to whisk her away. I was still awake when the milkman began his rounds, the sounds of the milk horse's clip-clop finally soothing me to sleep. When the alarm went at seven, I knew what to do.

Dear Mr Cowan,

70

Please excuse Louise Reid for the afternoon because she needs to bring her young brother to visit me in hospital as he is very upset by my illness.

Yours sincerely,

(Mrs) Katherine Reid

Mr Cowan, our Principal, was a bull with the heart of a new-born calf. Once at assembly when he was yelling at us, his false teeth fell out, and he started to laugh, as did all the teachers. However, when the kids got into the act, he resumed his bull-like persona and bellowed.

I arrived at Mum's ward at the Alfred Hospital a little before the afternoon visiting time and rang the ward bell. The same young nurse who was there the first time we came to see Mum opened the door. She couldn't let me in yet because Sister would have a 'conniption'.

'You look worried,' she said.

'My mother?' I almost didn't have the courage to ask.

'She's doing really well. Soon be right as rain. The doors will be opened in about five minutes.'

As I walked down the long ward toward Mum's bed, I saw her talking to a grey-haired man and, as I got closer, I realised he was wearing a dog-collar. I nearly panicked. What did it mean? Mum was surprised to see me, almost a little flustered. She introduced the man as Reverend Light, the minister of the church she went to. Reverend Light patted my mother's hand.

'Well, my dear, I'll come and see you when you're in the convalescent home. God bless.'

Convalescent home? We needed her at our home!

'It's good you're here by yourself, Lou. I need to tell you a few things.' She needed to get her health back, and the doctors had agreed she needed more time which was why she was going to the convalescent home for three weeks. Three weeks! Tears welled, threatening to spill. 'Darling, be brave. I have some good news.' What could make up for this blow? 'Guess who's coming to stay?'

71

'Not Grandma?'

'Yes,' Mum said, 'and she's staying for six weeks!'

17

My grandmother, Ruth Henderson, was a capable country woman who spoke her mind, as well as believing that she could tell what was happening in people's lives by the very first sniff of their home. She also believed that secrets had a smell like rotting fruit and melancholy smelt the same as a wet dog. I didn't really understand what she meant but as Grandma knew everything else, I believed her. She also said that 'being fond of a metaphor' she likened the stink of secrets and melancholy to snakes curled up sleeping. Snakes could be unpredictable, she said, because one year a boy had been bitten by a brown snake which should have been soundly asleep, then, sometime later, a neighbour had turned his shotgun on himself because he could not bear the weight of keeping secret from his wife the farm's coming bankruptcy. It was all a bit confusing but the cure for secrets and melancholy and snakes suddenly waking up was, according to Grandma, air and lots of it, air that could get into every nook and cranny.

So it was that two days after I'd visited Mum in hospital, when Johnno and I came home from school, every window of our house was flung up and the front and back doors held wide open with stacked books. Grandma had arrived! Looking through the open door I could see right through the house to the Norfolk Island pine in the back garden. That surely meant Grandma had smelt secrets and melancholy in our house. She hugged me tight. 'Why didn't you tell me, Lou?'

'I didn't know she took too many!'

'Of course she took too many – smell this place!' I couldn't smell anything but home.

My father sat in a lounge chair, shaved and hair slicked flat with Californian Poppy, drinking a cup of tea.

'Lou! Sit down and tell your father what you did at school today.' I did as I was told, having a proper conversation with Dad for the first time in ages. Grandma handed me a cup of tea and one of her prize-winning ginger biscuits. I asked where Johnno was.

'Where he should be at his age – playing with the little lad up the street – Paddy?'

'One of the O'Shanessy kids?' We never went near them – they were always dirty and swore at people.

'Mrs O'Shanessy's a lovely girl for all that she has too many babies. We must move with the times,' she added, either for her benefit or for mine, I wasn't sure.

'No alcohol in the house,' Grandma told Maggie, as she too was given a cup of tea and a ginger biscuit on her return from work. I was sure Maggie would protest, but after opening her mouth as if to speak, she thought better of it and promptly shut it again. A rare event.

'For Jack's sake,' Grandma added. 'He needs to get off the grog.'

Sitting as meekly as a visitor to a parsonage in a 19th century novel, Dad sipped his tea.

'The no grog ban also goes for ... um ... your ... our ... lodger ... Bill, I believe his name is. But of course what he does out of this house is his own business. As what you do is yours, my dear.'

My Grandma Henderson definitely should have been in charge of the world.

For the time she stayed with us, Grandma Henderson brought structure and optimism into our ragged household. Johnno regularly went off to play at Paddy's, even though Mum was afraid he'd catch head-lice. He didn't, but he did learn a lot of things he never knew before.

74

'Paddy's always saying, "Jesus wept", Lou. Isn't that bad? And he wees on the flowers too. He wees and then he laughs like a loon. But I like him still.'

However, when Paddy came to our house, he never made a peep except for 'Can I have a biscuit?' After he'd added the 'please', he was given it. He certainly wouldn't have dared wee on Dad's new vegie garden which, with Oldie's help, was coming along nicely.

When Mum came home from the convalescent hospital, she looked years younger, her care-worn expression only a faint shadow on her face. Our house smelt of fresh air and lavender, and sang with the chatter of Grandma and Mum and the hum of radio voices and music in the background, except when the serial *Blue Hills* was on, when silence reigned. Surprisingly, my parents were often together in soft conversation, and every afternoon Grandma sent them off for a walk while Johnno and I set the table. One of us had the job of getting a few flowers to put in the small vase on the table. Then, when Grandma said so, we all sat down to eat. Grandma believed that eating was always better if 'civil conversation' took place. She wasn't religious, but she believed we should be thankful for the food in front of us. Which is exactly what she said each evening: 'We are thankful for this food.' She added the 'Amen', she said, to round it off. If Bill was there he'd add, 'So say all of us' before tucking in. It was most fun when Bill had tea with us because somehow 'civil conversation' turned out to be hilarious.

18

The good times Grandma Henderson brought us came to an end and sooner than expected. Grandma's mother's sister, my Great-Great Aunt Lily, was a slightly unhinged woman who, we all knew, periodically 'took to the drink'. This was the polite way of saying that Great-Great Aunt Lily was an alcoholic, and the only reason she stayed sober these days was because she was very old with bad hips and Grandma had threatened 'retribution of a devilish kind' to every publican for miles around, as well as every neighbour, if they supplied her with anything stronger than ginger beer. Before Grandma came to Melbourne she'd made what she believed to be adequate arrangements for the care of Aunt Lily, but things suddenly went bad when the housekeeper had a family crisis and left Aunt Lily for an hour or two. When the housekeeper returned, she found Aunt Lily in 'a fine old state', according to Grandma.

'She called Tom, but he didn't know what to do. Pity Lily wasn't a cow, because then he'd have fixed her in no time.' Great-Uncle Tom was Grandma's brother who had a dairy farm on the Snowy River flood plains.

'Lily's seeing pink elephants.' Johnno and I were pop-eyed.

'Imagining things that aren't really there,' Grandma explained. 'I don't know how she got hold of it … a bottle of whisky! If I ever catch the swine who gave it to her! The way she's going, I'll have to put her in a home!'

'Wouldn't that be better?' I was thinking of poor Grandma.

'Certainly not! We're not a family that puts our own away.'

Before Grandma left the next morning to catch the train at Spencer Street Station, she took me aside.

'Now, Louise, I want you to ring me if ... and make sure your mother doesn't take any of those damn pills. I wish I lived closer ... You must tell me if you need me, your mother ... she battles on ... but ... she was always such a dreamer ... Promise me you'll let me know...' The very last thing Grandma said to me was, 'Keep the windows open!'

I wanted to say, 'Stay, please stay, we need you still!' But what about Aunt Lily and her drinking, and Uncle Tom who was lonely and couldn't cook, as well as Grandma's old cocker spaniel, Foolish, who pined when she was away? I wanted to say, 'How will I know if Mum's alright, what can I do about Dad?' I wanted to say, 'Don't go! I'm too young to know what I need to know.' In the book, *Caddie,* that Bill had given me, Caddie was a heroine but a heroine in the hardest way, not even getting true love in the end. She'd come down so low, working in smelly, rat-infested bars, being hungry and cold and having packing cases to sit on instead of proper chairs. Her story was more frightening because it was real, and because it was real I knew it could happen, even to us.

The routines that Grandma imposed on us kept our household afloat for weeks after her departure and we might have even gone for months without any major disruption, but for the break-up of Maggie and Bill. Bill's daughter, who I'd barely thought of, because it seemed Bill never did, and whose name I now learned was Anne, was diagnosed with leukaemia. Bill was distraught, and told Maggie that he must return to the family home to care for her. Maggie didn't want him to go, and said he could help out just as well from where he was. Over an increasingly bitter few weeks, they fought it out. Maggie, never one to hold back, certainly didn't now. Bill was a bastard and a liar. He'd used her. He loved his daughter

77

more than he loved her. He really wanted to get back with his wife! His daughter's illness was an excuse to break off with Maggie. Much of this happened within our earshot. In her distress, Maggie became ugly in every way. Part of me didn't blame Bill for wanting to get rid of such a harridan, and yet I'd seen and heard how much she was in love with him. Poor Maggie. What a strange and terrible thing this passion was. The earth may have moved for them once, but now something far less pleasant was in place. Bill's set jaw told of his distress.

'Couldn't he stay with Maggie and still help his daughter?' I asked Mum.

'It's complicated, Lou. Maggie's always made light of Bill's family, which was a big mistake, because family ties are very hard to break.'

'But Bill doesn't love his wife. He loves Maggie!'

'There's different kinds of love, even between a man and woman,' Mum said.

I didn't understand what she meant. Didn't you fall in love with one person and *know* that person was the only one for you? Surely any other kind of love for another man or woman was impossible?

She tried to explain: 'Often, when a tragedy happens like this, people are forced to come down on one side or the other. That's what's happening to Bill now. We're in for a bumpy ride.'

Soon, all the windows in our house remained closed.

19

Already, at fourteen, I'd wearied of the inevitability of good times turning to bad but I'd never given up hope because even when things seemed blackest, I was still able to imagine a future – my own. A future when I would be free, and life, unlike my father's, mother's, Maggie's or even Bill's, would go my way.

Although my home was full of Maggie's bitter grieving and its fall-out, I concentrated on the Japanese garden and my fledgling love life. I constantly daydreamed of Toluk taking my hand, of him holding me close to his body and me drowning in his remarkable eyes, et cetera, but the reality was that, since the day at the pictures, no more than exchanged glances, blushes, a few smiles and the occasional hello had occurred. There was surely a stage or two between the current reality and my daydream but how to make that leap? Toluk was always surrounded by kids who wanted to be his friend, or more, like Rosemary Smith, who smiled at him so much she was at risk of damaging her facial muscles. Libby said he liked me, and she knew about boys. My other friend at school, Jenny, who was more serious, but really smart, thought so too. But I wasn't at all sure. If he did, why didn't he come over and talk to me? I always hung around the area he was in during recess and lunch. All he needed to do was walk over to me. In the end, literature helped. All those heroines who waited for a sign, then misread it, all those Jane Austen characters who couldn't tell like from dislike, friendship from love. Thinking about these fictional people somehow made me braver. Could it be that Toluk didn't cross the quadrangle to speak to me because he was shy and scared that I might reject him? Well, I wasn't an 18th or 19th century woman who had to wait for her man – Maria from *For Whom the Bells Toll* was a 20th century woman and she certainly hadn't held back, so neither would I!

I'd like to say I marched boldly up to Toluk, but the reality was, I sidled up to him, slowly altering my position until the distance between us was very short. Perhaps that gave him courage, because as I walked toward him in what I hoped was a nonchalant manner, he moved in my direction. It was magic. It was, I was pretty sure, almost as good as the earth moving.

Suddenly, I was one of a couple, a couple that every kid at school and probably every teacher knew about. We were inseparable, and every day was an adventure in this delightful new world I now inhabited. I was the girlfriend of a handsome, exotic boy who was one of the most popular boys at school. Other boys, who had never before deigned to glance at me, now sought me out. 'Desire', how I loved that word, just as my best-loved books had desire at their heart. As I'd seen with Maggie, desire had the power to transform. For the first time, I looked at myself in the mirror with pleasure, not criticism. When did my hair get to be so shiny and a bit film-star-ish? Even my small breasts, long a reason of discontent, even though Mum had told me it was better to have rosebuds than great big cabbages, now seemed pert and pretty. And my eyes – how could I not have noticed how unusual their hazel colour was? For the first time ever, seeing myself through a lover's eyes, I was adorable, and so, despite the other side of a love affair being played out in my home, I remained as light as air, as untouchable as a cloud.

After seeing the books Hanaka had borrowed from the municipal library, I too began to take the tram ride there twice a week. Johnno came with me every Thursday after school. It was not so much that I'd grown tired of our Library Man's often tatty books, but that Toluk and I could spend an hour or two away from the prying eyes of school mates and, if we browsed the shelves furthest away from the librarian's desk, we could indulge ourselves in considerably more touching and kissing than we could at school. On Thursdays, when Johnno went with me, I left him in the section where the children's books were kept. He was becoming an avid reader like Mum and me, so while Toluk and I petted, Johnno never stirred from the spot where I had left him. Or so I believed.

One of Toluk's charms for me was that he was older – sixteen – but because of the language problem, he was kept in a lower form. I began to find that this charm was also a problem – Toluk was a physically mature boy – a man. His insistent mouth, his insistent hand that always found its way to cup my breast or to slide up to the silky smoothness of my thigh before lingering at the elastic of my underpants filled me with both fear and excitement. I would then attempt to still his shockingly insistent fingers because I knew what happened to girls who went too far. But oh, how I wanted to!

One afternoon Toluk persuaded me to go down to the creek with him and when we got there he asked me to take off my clothes and let him lie next to me. To be so desired was intoxicating. He promised he wouldn't do anything but still I insisted I keep my underpants on. Toluk's hard penis and his increasingly ragged breath suddenly frightened me and I tried to push him away but I couldn't. I finally understood how easy it was to go all the way or, rather, how hard not to. As he rubbed against me making anguished noises he kept me in a firm grip and then all at once there was wetness on my pants and legs. I didn't know what to think: I didn't know if it was nice or horrible.

But I should have known from my reading that, although lovers are oblivious to those around them, nothing is more potently obvious than lovers. One afternoon I came home from the library to find my mother and my father sitting stiffly on the lounge chairs waiting, waiting, I understood after a moment's confusion, for me.

81

Word had got back to my mother about Toluk and me. She never said from whom. Johnno had also told her he'd seen me and Toluk kissing in the library. He wouldn't tell her how many times, so she assumed it was more than once. It wasn't Johnno's fault he'd told, she'd made him. He was very upset about the whole affair. She didn't accuse me of doing anything wrong with the boy, although she was very hurt that I'd deceived them. What about my reputation, too, being seen carrying on in the public library? 'I didn't bring you up to behave like this, Louise,' Mum said in a sorrowful way. She wasn't against the boy, she said, but she was told he was very mature; that he'd grown up in a farming community and he'd experienced war. Here my mother hesitated, finally settling on, 'he knows so much more than you about the world' adding again that he was far too mature. She and Dad were sorry, but I was not allowed to continue seeing him. I must tell Toluk this tomorrow, but if he didn't take any notice, the school would tell him. Where could this relationship lead? I was far too young. My father, nodding agreement with Mum, said his only words on the subject.

'You don't want to be getting into trouble, Louise. Your whole future would be ruined.'

We all knew what he was talking about.

Mum warned me that if I didn't do as I was told, she'd have to get Grandma. I would rather have died than have Grandma disappointed with me, so I agreed to what my parents demanded, but not quietly. I cried for hours, then I stormed. How could they be so unfair? I was old enough! They didn't want me to be with Toluk because he was foreign (which my mother vehemently denied, but the truth was, in real life, she did find some sorts of foreign quite alarming). They cared more about what horrible old gossips thought than they did about me. They didn't want me to be happy.

'Lou, sooner or later it would end unhappily,' Mum said. 'Look at Maggie.'

'That's because Bill's married,' I retorted. Didn't she know *anything*?

82

'Bill's married. You're too young. Same thing.'

When Maggie came home, banging through the house in her ferocious bitterness, I took to my bedroom to sob quietly.

'What's the matter with her?' I heard her ask Mum.

'Just a friendship quarrel,' Mum replied. None of us wanted to get Maggie in on the act. Johnno didn't escape for his part in my undoing either. 'Traitor,' I hissed at him every time no one else was in earshot. Even though his eyes brimmed with tears, he didn't tell on me.

I hated them all and determined I'd leave school as soon as I turned fifteen. I'd get a job and save up and as soon as I could I'd … I'd leave ... and … and I'd get married, forgetting that I'd decided marriage was not up to much, but at least I'd be away from them and they wouldn't be able to stop me doing what I wanted. I'd get away, I would!

I wrote Toluk a letter, which I gave him at lunchtime. I told him I'd always love him, but it was not meant to be. He said when he was older he'd come and take me away. We embraced passionately. Less than a month later, Libby told me Toluk had been seen with a girl with a reputation for going 'all the way'. I was spared the ignominy of having to see them together, because she went to a Catholic school.

In my secret heart, I was relieved – although loving being desired and the feeling of wanting to go all the way, the reality of what that meant, the physiology of the sexual act, was no longer a hazy fantasy. In some of the novels I'd read, two characters embrace with great passion and intent, but the writer, not up to the actual sex, cheats by inserting an * followed by a scene where the heroine, radiating sexual satiation, languidly sips her morning cup of tea. My experience with Toluk down by the creek had given me a real idea of what sex was, but realising that I didn't yet want to go all the way or even a good part of the way, I'd avoided repeating it, even as Toluk became more insistent. Although my parents deemed me 'too young' for actions far more innocent than those I'd actually experienced, I wasn't about to tell them that.

When Johnno and I were friends again, he said he was glad I'd been found out. Apparently, he'd become skilled at spying on Toluk and me.

'You two kissed like buggers.' Johnno's friendship with Paddy O'Shanessy had added to his vocabulary, but I was the only one he dared try the new words out on.

'Like Aunt Maggie and Bill. I didn't tell Mum that. I only said I'd seen you kissing. I didn't want you to get like Aunt Maggie.' His dear little face screwed up with distaste.

'What's kissing feel like?'

'When you're grown-up you'll like it,' I said.

'You're not grown-up yet, either, Lou,' Johnno told me.

20

While involved in my grand passion with Toluk, I had somewhat neglected Hanaka. When I did call in to see her, it was often only for a very short time. Now that I was free again, I wanted to pick up where we had left off, but I found that something had changed for Hanaka. Her Quaker neighbour had found a painter who'd agreed to give Hanaka lessons. Hanaka was very happy about this, and so was I, as it had been my suggestion in the first place, but as the weeks went by, whenever I went to her house I'd find her engrossed in her work. At first, I loved to see the way she painted light strokes, magically resembling hills or rivers, in the gentlest of colours. I loved too, knowing that painting made her happy but, one afternoon, the day we always read *The Women's Weekly* together, Hanaka told me that she must keep on with her painting because her teacher wanted her to finish it by the next week. It came as a real shock, followed by a frightening sense of desolation. Hanaka didn't want to stop painting and spend time with me! In a sudden panic, I burst into tears. As Hanaka worriedly comforted me, I explained that my mother was still sick. Not quite a total lie, since Mum was not yet fully well, but a bended truth used to manipulate. It worked. Hanaka put aside her painting and spent her time making me feel better, better because she was taking notice of me.

Although she put her painting aside for me that day, she didn't always do so, and I had too much pride to cry again to get her attention. But I was desperate to have Hanaka back in my domain and, in order to achieve this, I reasoned, our Japanese garden needed to get up and running.

Every time we met I talked about the garden and gathered new ideas between visits – some from reading old gardening manuals, some so fanciful as to be ridiculous – but always with the single intention of never being without enthusiasm for our project. Unfortunately, Alan was a major impediment to my plans – he was always tired at the weekend, unable to find the strength to do the necessary digging. What a pansy! My father used that word sometimes; it was like calling a man a sissy, but worse. It fitted Hanaka's husband well. If only I could use Oldie. He'd have the garden dug up in no time.

I'll never know whether I wore Hanaka into submission or whether she really wanted to go ahead with the garden, but one afternoon when I arrived at her house, she greeted me with some wonderful words: 'You would like to see the plan I have made for our garden?' She unrolled a cylinder of white paper and laid it on the table, placing stone tortoise paperweights at its corners to prevent it re-rolling. Before my eyes was our garden delicately drawn in black ink.

'The vista is from the kitchen window and sunroom,' Hanaka explained. 'We will contain it on both sides by fencing. In Japan, this would be bamboo, but if not, we could plant bamboo in front of a wooden fence. Here, on both sides of a path that winds a little, will be azaleas. On this side, we will make a hill and place rocks and a tree, a maple, mature but not too tall. The camellia tree already in the garden is this one here. Then, Lou, you will look to the back. Do you remember about the Japanese gardening technique called *shakkei*, "borrowed landscape", where something in the landscape outside the garden is used as part of the garden's design?'

I remembered that quite clearly, and nodded.

'So, what do you think we will borrow for our garden?'

It took me a second and then I knew!

'The old apple tree! But ... but is it in the rules?' I asked Hanaka.

'I cannot see that there is any difference between borrowing a pagoda or borrowing this tree. Yes, in the rules – *our* rules!'

21

Although my parents rallied together to deal with my misbehaviour, Maggie's situation pulled them both down. She'd begun drinking heavily at night, sherry as well as beer, and her unhappiness turned to vitriol. No one was safe from it. The absent Bill got most of it, but so did men in general and wives too, being parasites as far as Maggie was concerned. As well as fools.

'Don't think you'll ever find true lurrv,' she'd say, stretching the word into a term of mockery.

'Men only want one thing and they'll take it whenever they can.' Somehow, she'd caught wind that I'd had a boyfriend, and when we were alone which, despite my best efforts, sometimes happened, she'd bait me by saying things like, 'Bet you got up to more than you told your mother.'

One night, she said, 'Your mother's such a stupid innocent. You've really pulled the wool over her eyes, Miss butter-doesn't-melt-in-your-mouth. But you don't fool me. I know what you get up to ...'

For one heart-stopping moment I thought she'd found out about Hanaka. 'Shut your mouth,' I shouted.

Maggie was up out of her chair and by my side in a flash. 'What did you just say?' She grabbed hold of my arm. I pulled away from her, upsetting the small table with her glass of beer on it. 'You little bitch! Without me propping you all up, you'd be out on the street!' Her face was so hateful she frightened me, but I couldn't put up with her poison any more.

'You're a bitter old maid and I'm glad Bill left you!'

The words were barely out when a blow hit my cheek. I pushed her backwards and she stumbled as I picked up a chair, ready to defend myself. Suddenly, both Mum and Dad were in the room, pale with shock, and then Johnno began to scream.

'Get your hands off her!' It was Dad. 'What the bloody hell do you think you're doing, Maggie?'

Mum, who had been standing, stunned, near the doorway came to and put her arm around my shoulder. 'Go to your room, Lou, and take Johnno with you.'

'It was her fault,' Maggie shouted. 'The little bitch!'

'Shut up!' Dad shouted back at her. I didn't want to go to my room because I was frightened things would get even more out of control than they were now.

'Go on, Louise,' Mum said, 'Do what I've asked you.'

Johnno dragged at my hand, pulling me away. My little brother was as white as a ghost. I kept a packet of Jaffas – orange-coloured balls filled with dark chocolate – for emergencies and as this was surely one, I got them out from my hiding place. Johnno and I silently ate the entire packet as our parents' and Maggie's loud and unhappy voices continued in the lounge room. Then we heard the front door slam and there was silence. Mum came to my room and, after getting Johnno to go and make Dad a cup of tea, she asked me whether I'd told Maggie that I was glad Bill had left her. I said yes, but only because she was saying awful things to me.

'That was very unkind of you, Louise.' I was dumbfounded. 'Maggie's absolutely heartbroken about Bill, and she's drinking far too much. I'm worried she might harm herself.'

Did Mum mean Maggie might put her head in the gas oven? Jump off Princes Bridge into the Yarra River? *Throw herself under a train like Anna Karenina*? Women did extreme things because of love, I knew, but I'd found Anna hard to understand, killing herself over the worthless Vronsky. Poor old Bill wasn't a Vronsky, but what if Maggie? I started to cry.

'It's alright Pet, it's not your fault. Maggie's impossible at the moment. She's threatened to sell the house. Your father's terribly upset. I simply don't know what to do.'

Sell the house! Where would we go? Maggie wouldn't! Would she?

'To be honest, I'd love to live somewhere else,' Mum said, 'Maybe go back home, be near Mum. I'd love to have my own home ... but Jack ... I think it would make him worse. You might have to apologise, Lou.'

Poor Mum! There and then I vowed to myself that I would never apologise, even if it meant the house was sold, because Mum would be happier in another house, even if it was smaller, and then none of us would ever have to put up with Maggie again! But that night I tossed and turned worrying that we might have to leave our lovely old house and its garden and how sad that would make Dad and how sad I would be too. I couldn't even bear to think about leaving Hanaka.

In the morning, grumpy and miserable from worry and lack of sleep, I went into the kitchen to make breakfast. Through the kitchen window I could see Mum talking to Oldie in the garden. It seemed a tense sort of conversation – what was it about? Mum came into the house, and I realised for the first time that she looked much older than when she'd first come back from the convalescent home.

'Oldie says Maggie's a bully and like all bullies needs to be stood up to. He says I should tell her that I've contacted the real estate agent to put the house on the market.'

'But ... but what if ... if she thinks that's a good thing?'

'At least we'll know where we stand.'

Maggie didn't come home that night or the next. We all sweated it out, wondering what would happen and, then on the third day, she returned home from work at her usual time.

'Hello,' she said to Mum, ignoring me. I buried my head deep in my book and kept very, very still.

90

'Hello, Maggie,' Mum replied. 'The real estate agent's coming around early tomorrow evening to value the house.' Mum gave a great performance.

'Best to get it over and done with, better for Jack, don't you think?'

It seemed Maggie didn't know what to think, or say. She quickly left the kitchen without uttering a word. About an hour later, just before tea time, she came back into the kitchen.

'Can I speak to you privately?' she asked Mum, not looking at me, but meaning without me.

'Of course, Maggie. Lou, off you go. Tea will be ready in fifteen minutes.'

I longed to give Maggie a dirty look, but didn't dare. When Johnno and I came into the kitchen for tea, Maggie was chatting away to Dad, and Mum had a very strange expression on her face – not sad, but not happy either. Her expression was rather like Grandma Henderson's whenever she exclaimed, 'God give me strength!' My family. I would never understand them. I was not asked to apologise, and I certainly didn't volunteer. Maggie and I mostly managed to pretend the other wasn't there.

A few days later, I saw Oldie, and he called me over. 'Girlie, I want ya to listen to me.' What was he going to tell me? 'I'm speaking out of turn, I know, but watch out for ya aunt. She's a great hater, always has been, and ya need to keep out of her way. Understand me, Girlie?'

I knew I should heed Oldie's warning, but I would not be instructed.

22

No more was said about Maggie's threat, but the recent events seemed to have unsettled the house itself. First, a huge downpour revealed new leaks in the roof which required every bucket and bowl in the household. Then the lavatory blocked and the plumber spent two days digging to fix it. As if this wasn't enough, small things like hinges, door knobs, light switches and window sashes sequentially gave up the ghost. My father made some attempt to fix these, but his concentration was poor and, as often as not, he gave up. Mum got a local man in who did a reasonable job, but it was stop-gap stuff. The house was old and urgently needed attention, including a paint job inside and out, but we didn't have the money for any of that because the plumber's bill had used up all the money in the emergencies envelope. Mum budgeted by this envelope system: wood, electricity, milk, clothing, Christmas and even the Library Man all had their own envelopes which were kept in an old chocolate box behind the flour jar in the pantry. Maggie had paid some money toward the plumber's bill, but her arrangement with Mum and Dad was that they pay for most repairs as they used the house the most. I pointed out that as nothing major had been done to the house since Grandma and Grandpa were alive, this was bad arithmetic, but Mum said now wasn't the time to argue the toss with Maggie. When things settled down, she said, she'd try and bring up the subject.

Money and its inability to stretch the required distance was a constant worry for both my mother and me, but like all young girls I wanted to look nice and fit in with my friends. Fortunately, my mother was a good seamstress, as was Grandma Henderson and, because of their skills, I always managed to look like a fashionable Miss. But that winter, with no money left in the emergencies envelope, Mum said I'd have to make do with the clothes I already owned, as she needed to save what she could. I understood, but it made me angry that Maggie had new clothes and shoes, yet Mum had to wear the same old things, and I couldn't even have a new winter skirt. To add insult to injury, walking past a shoe shop in the larger shopping centre near the library where Toluk and I used to meet, I saw the most gorgeous pair of ruby-coloured shoes, complete with a ribbon bow and a very small heel, displayed in the window. I wanted them! It was as if my entire future depended on being able to possess those shoes, but I knew I couldn't, I shouldn't, even ask Mum if I could have them. Even if we'd had the money, Mum would probably have told me the shoes were both far too grown-up and the colour impractical. Could I ask Grandma Henderson? No, I couldn't do that, as I'd guessed she was already supplying money to my household. In short, I shouldn't even think about owning the shoes, but that didn't stop me coveting them fiercely. Then I had a brilliant idea. I had a precious 8 shillings squirrelled away for birthday and Christmas gifts, but if I used 5 shillings of that money to put down a first lay-by payment then – trying to convince myself of the possibility of the impossible – all I'd have to do was find the money to continue making fortnightly payments over several months.

Dying to tell Hanaka about my dream shoes, I knocked on her door as usual. Normally Hanaka opened the door within moments, but on this day nothing happened. I knocked again, harder, and about thirty seconds or so passed before I heard her coming to the door. The Hanaka who opened the door was as white as one of Grandma's newly bleached sheets.

'I am not well, Louise,' she said. I could see that!

'I must rest, so it is best ...' Before she could finish her sentence, she made a strange sound and, with her hand over her mouth, hurried toward the lavatory. I took this opportunity to go into the house and put the kettle on. Hanaka came back more greenish than white, and sat down on the couch.

'I'll make you a cup of tea,' I said.

'Thank you, but I do not think ...'

'Weak black tea with lots of sugar. It's really good for a stomach bug.'

'I do not think I can ...'

'How long have you been sick?' I asked. 'Have you been to the doctor?'

'I am fine ... The doctor said ...' Then poor Hanaka was off to the lavatory again. When she returned, she staggered me by saying, 'This is normal.' Normal? What on earth was she talking about?

'I am sorry Louise, but I must go to my room and lie down.'

Disappointed at not being able to tell Hanaka about the shoes, I was dawdling homewards, trying to work out a scheme to get the money for the lay-by payments, when I stopped in my tracks. No, I hadn't had a sudden brainwave as to how I'd get the needed money, but rather a lightning bolt of realisation: when Hanaka said, 'This is normal', she didn't mean that a pale face and frequent trips to the lavatory was normal; what she meant was, it was normal to experience such sickness when one was going to have a baby! A baby!

I was over the moon. I wanted to run back to Hanaka's place and tell her so, but I didn't. I hoped Alan would come home early from work to look after her and show all the gentle kindness of an Edward Ferrars but, as well, the authority of a Mr Darcy in keeping Mother McDonald at bay. No! What was really needed was a Colonel Brandon. Why hadn't I considered him before? He had the maturity that Edward lacked, as well as having no mother, and he was as independent as Mr Darcy without his damned pride! He would have brought Mother McDonald to heel, quick smart. Alas, there was only Alan, and I feared for Hanaka.

After Alan and I decided we must never see each other again, two weeks passed, two very long weeks. Then, one afternoon I found Alan waiting for me, holding a beautifully wrapped gift. I did not know it at the time, but Alan's gift was the obi that I would wear on our wedding day. All I knew was that the man who gave it to me was a man who I did not want to leave my life. The obi itself told me that Alan too had decided that he did not want to let me go: the embroidered decoration of camellia and bamboo with snow on the leaves and flowers signifies to Japanese people the resilience of nature's life force. We became lovers that night.

'It'll be hard, Hanaka,' Alan had said. 'So hard that sometimes you'll wish you'd never met me.'

I refused to believe that it could ever be that hard or that I would ever want to be without him.

'I'll always look after you. If something or someone hurts you, they'll have me to answer to.'

But it was hard, hard to be alone together, hard not to make love because of the fear of a baby who would be reviled, hard that people whispered about women like me, saying we only went with the foreigners so that we would be given food and gifts and that we were no better than prostitutes. So hard waiting, waiting to get the permission to come to Australia. Although Alan always tried to look after me he too was powerless in many ways. We both clung on to our dream that when we got to Australia everything would come right.

23

Prunus blossom heralded early spring, even as a cold Melbourne wind made us pull our coats tightly around us. At Hanaka's, the old apple tree, the 'borrowed landscape' for our planned garden, showed small signs that, in due course, it would became a riot of flower, but the garden it was to enhance remained untouched and forlorn, except for a small clump of jonquils.

Unlike the jonquils, Hanaka definitely wasn't blooming at this stage. She was pale and, unable to keep much down, had become very thin. But despite this, I could see she was happy. Mother McDonald arranged for her to have the baby in a small private hospital, with the local GP to deliver. My mother had given birth to me and my brother in the same hospital. Hanaka said she would have to stay there for two weeks.

'Why is this necessary, Louise?' she asked me. I didn't have a clue, but I asked Mum, who said giving birth was an exhausting business, and that a woman needed time to rest afterwards, and to learn how to look after her new baby. Hanaka told me that in Japan it was the custom for a pregnant woman to return to her parents' home for the delivery, and afterwards to be looked after by her mother, or sisters, who would prepare her strengthening foods and also care for the newborn baby. 'It is lucky I am in Australia,' Hanaka said, 'because in Japan there would be no one to look after me.'

What about her aunt and cousins? Wouldn't they have looked after her? As if reading my mind, Hanaka continued, 'When I told my aunt that Alan and I were to marry, she ... I am no longer welcome ...'

Good riddance to bad rubbish, I thought. Poor Hanaka. Here, she would have the loneliness of being amongst strangers in the hospital and, when she got home, Mother McDonald would be sticking her nasty nose in. 'I'll help you, Hanaka, I promise.' Hanaka gave me a gentle smile, replete with regret and acceptance. It made my heart ache.

My joy makes me brave enough to expose delicate memories of my own mother, memories long locked away for fear the world's harshness could ruin them. Now I can almost smell her scent, hear her praise, even the way she sometimes scolded. I imagine she is once more joking with the noodle seller, her concentration as she prepares food for a festive meal, her face when she is in prayer ... the way she smiled at my father's stories ... these cherished images I now allow myself, take into myself, re-live, so I can become a mother to my child as my own dearest mother was to me.

If my life was different ... but that is not my karma, so I do not linger on what cannot be. I am at once afraid of what is to come, yet welcome it, walk toward it – no, I run toward it trembling yet as fearless as a lioness.

Although my attachment to Hanaka became even more intense with her pregnancy, her world continued to expand. The painting lessons brought her into contact with a number of artists, and even the neighbours began to warm to her, not to mention her Quaker friend and that circle. As well, she and another war bride had connected through their husbands knowing each other, and Hanaka and this woman met every second week in each other's homes, and sometimes went out in the evening to the pictures with their husbands. Although jealous of Hanaka's new friends, I knew how to keep that hidden from her.

In light of Hanaka's expanding world, I felt I needed to work very hard to keep her attention. In my mind, our planned garden became an even more important project, but working on our garden was now out of the question for Hanaka, who treated herself very gingerly, and most often had her hand over the place where her baby grew. Alan it seemed, while too fatigued to dig the garden, was quite strong enough to begin painting the spare room which would become the nursery. I clung to the belief that our planned Japanese garden was the alchemy necessary to bind Hanaka and secure my place in her life, but it seemed that it was going to be up to me to do something about it. What exactly, I was at a loss to know.

24

It was during one of our big cleanups that the idea first came to me. These cleanups happened when our household became unworkable because we'd run out of clean teacups and nobody could find the book, the purse, the jumper, or whatever else it was they needed. My job was to tidy the lounge room, picking up and putting away all belongings that didn't live there, dusting the ornaments, including the photo of my father in the silver frame, and then vacuuming with our second-hand Hoover, which was extremely temperamental. Mum usually went into Maggie's room to collect cups, ashtrays and old newspapers as we were not supposed to go there, but on this day she told Johnno to do it. Carrying a few precariously balanced cups from Maggie's room, Johnno asked, 'Mum? What will I do with the money she's dropped on the floor?'

'Leave it exactly where it is,' Mum told him, 'and don't touch anything else, either.'

Later, as I scrubbed out scum from the bottom of cups from Maggie's room, I had a very clear thought: it wasn't fair of Maggie to carelessly strew her spare change over the floor when she lived with a family who had no spare change. This thought was followed by a conviction of equal clarity: I was going to steal some of Maggie's unwanted money.

Now, of course I knew that stealing was wrong, although I'd always considered it perfectly understandable if a person was hungry or thirsty or needed money to save a life. Grandma Henderson said we had a couple of convict ancestors who'd been sentenced in England to transportation to Tasmania, which was called Van Diemen's Land then, for stealing bread and a dress. 'That's why we're a tough bunch,' Grandma told me. 'If you didn't die in overcrowded prison hulks waiting to be transported, nor on the ship coming over which took about six months, or from the hard labour and whippings when you got here, you could survive just about anything.' Grandma was very proud of 'our convicts' whereas most people thought it something shameful to admit to, and preferred to claim descent from the landed gentry.

To justify my actions, I constructed a kind of adventure story in which I was rather like my convict forebears, forced by need and by the greed of others – the 'others' being Maggie – to take what was necessary to survive but despite my best efforts, I couldn't quite convince myself. I turned to another source, and what better source than a heroine who would easily commit such an act as mine – and far worse. Hanaka and I were reading a very old copy of *Vanity Fair* that I'd found amongst the Library Man's offerings and Becky Sharp's actions made us gasp with both shock and pleasure. I asked Mr Birch, our English teacher who was about to retire after being a teacher forever, how he would describe Becky Sharp. Mr Birch raised one bushy eyebrow. 'Becky Sharp? My, my, Louise Reid, you'll get yourself into trouble reading books like that.' He always said strange things. 'I'll give you one word for Becky Sharp. *Amoral*. Look it up in a dictionary, but you won't understand it until you're about thirty-five.' I did look it up – also, *immoral* – which caused me even more confusion because I couldn't quite understand the difference. My actions were justified, I reasoned, because Maggie obviously cared nothing about the money she dropped, and as an amoral – or immoral – action, Becky Sharp would laugh at the smallness of my crime. Having already paid my precious shillings as down-payment for the shoes, and with the next payment due in ten

100

days' time, I needed to get going fast. But first I needed to talk to my little brother.

Johnno was a fossicker, always on the look-out for what he called treasures such as buttons, coloured glass, pieces of rock or metal, feathers, fragments of material – anything at all that took his fancy. It was Grandma Henderson who first called him a bowerbird. Each year satin bowerbirds came to where she lived, and although you hardly ever saw the mature blue-black male, the brown and green female and younger males caused havoc in people's vegetable gardens. The males collected treasures to decorate their bower of twigs and, as each species of bowerbird collected items in their own colour range, the mature satin bowerbird collected mainly blue objects, even clothes pegs, then arranged their treasures in an exceedingly complex way, even noticing if in their absence from their bower, an item had been moved. If so, the bowerbird would move the item back to its original position. Johnno behaved in a similar manner: his bower was the top shelf of his rather shabby brown bookcase, and he would spend hours arranging the things he found, often talking to himself as he did so. No one was allowed to touch the items he arranged and, once when I did so to tease him, he became incredibly upset. I never did it again, because it distressed him so. When he'd been younger, we'd all thought his bowerbird tendencies endearing, but now Mum and Grandma were worried about Johnno's attachment to his bower shelf. Various schemes were tried to wean Johnno away but he was never distracted for long. Mum thought he'd grow out of it in time but Grandma was not so optimistic.

When Johnno had asked Mum what to do about Maggie's carelessly dropped change, I shrewdly guessed that he visited Maggie's room at times other than when Mum told him to collect cups, and that he would have explored every nook and cranny in the room, maybe even taking a treasure or two. I asked Johnno how much money had been on Maggie's floor: I knew he would have counted it.

101

'Three and six pence,' he said. 'That's a lot, isn't it, Lou?'

I agreed it was – to us anyhow – and, I suggested, Maggie must be quite rich, to drop that amount of money on her floor.

'She's very rich,' he whispered.

'How do you know?' I asked.

'I just know,' he said, trying to back out of the trap I'd set.

'Tell me,' I said. 'It'll be our secret.'

'I haven't done anything wrong, Lou.'

'I know that!'

'I was looking for a treasure, you know, something ... not money ... and ... and I found it ... the envelope ...'

'You're like Sherlock Holmes,' I said. He beamed.

'I don't know how much is in it, I didn't count it or anything or she would have known, but it's a lot.'

'How do you know that, if you haven't counted it?'

'It's thick, like ...' Johnno indicated about one and half inches. 'How come Aunt Maggie's rich, Lou, but we're not?'

How come indeed!

'Doesn't she ever pick up the money she drops?' I asked.

'Sometimes it's all cleared away, but then there's more.'

I wasted no time. The next morning after Maggie left for work and while the rest of the family were busy getting ready for the day, I ducked into her room. The room smelt of stale cigarettes and the rose talcum powder Maggie used, and on the floor, just as Johnno had said, were pennies and half-pennies and a couple of sixpences. I looked further, and found a shilling at the back of the dressing table. I quickly pocketed it, as well as a penny, and left the room. It was so easy.

102

25

Emboldened by my success as a thief, I became determined to also solve the problem of turning the hard earth of Hanaka's garden into well-turned soil ready for planting. I'd thought of asking for Oldie's help a few times before but, because I feared my secret relationship would be exposed, I'd always rejected the idea pretty quickly. Now, I decided, Oldie was the only one to get that garden dug, and all I needed to do was to come up with a very good story to get him to agree to dig as well as getting him to dig when Hanaka was not around.

As it happened, Mother Nature, as Grandma called it, appeared to favour the bold too, blowing up a storm which damaged some of our trees and had Oldie around at our place by half past seven in the morning.

'Bugger of a storm,' Oldie stated. 'Get ya Dad out here to help ... Go on, Girlie!'

'I've got a friend who needs her garden dug, the back garden,' I blurted, 'but her husband's got ... got a broken leg ... and she ... my friend ... is having a baby... and so ...' A broken leg? I couldn't believe I'd said that!

'Two quid,' Oldie said.

Two quid? Stupidly, I hadn't even thought about paying Oldie. I didn't know what to say.

'One and half, but that's the best I can do. Gotta keep Pamela and Pepe in fuel. Now, get ya Dad.'

I flirted briefly with the idea of telling Oldie to keep it between ourselves, but as he was a man of few words I decided to take the chance he wouldn't mention our conversation to either of my parents.

In this first flush of enthusiasm, I put the plan to Hanaka who thought it very good and was happy to pay Oldie. It would be a surprise for Alan, she said, as he worried about never getting around to the garden. Worried about, but never bloody doing it! But I didn't say that. Hanaka wanted the garden dug as soon as possible, but I told her Oldie was busy and probably couldn't come for a couple of weeks, as I was beginning to fear the whole idea was a bit rash. If it did go ahead, one thing was for sure: when Oldie dug up the garden, Hanaka and Alan must be elsewhere.

Strangely, behaving rashly was not something I'd considered when pocketing Maggie's small change. I'd convinced myself that taking what Maggie was so careless about was justified in a Becky Sharp sort of way. *Half* convinced really, because I knew it was wrong, and that Maggie had every right to do with her own money whatever she chose. It was the arrogance of what she chose that got to me – carelessly dropping money that we could have made good use of – and overcame any qualms of conscience. I convinced myself that my wrong was less than Maggie's, and, as well, it was so easy to do, slipping into her room and swiftly picking up a penny, a sixpence and occasionally a one shilling piece. No one noticed a thing. But my success made me, like Maggie, arrogant, and I forgot that old saying about throwing a pebble into a pond and causing ripples way beyond the harmless small pebble you first held in your hand.

Should I allow Oldie to dig up Hanaka's garden, taking the chance that he wouldn't start asking awkward questions or find out whose garden it was? If I did so, Hanaka's garden would be ready for planting and, with this joint project underway, I would be assured of a secure place in her life. But what of possible complications? Like Oldie finding out, and telling my mother? Oldie mightn't say much, but he noticed

104

everything. Anyhow, for it to be even possible, Hanaka and Alan must be somewhere else for at least a whole day while Oldie dug, and as that seemed unlikely to happen in the short term, I still had time to think about whether it was wise to involve Oldie in what must be kept a secret.

Everything changed when Hanaka announced that she and Alan, her friend, Naoko, and Naoko's husband were all going on a trip to Sydney. They would be gone for two weeks. Now all of Hanaka's talk was of the Sydney Harbour Bridge, Hyde Park, ferry trips and the clothes she and Naoko would wear when they went to these places. I felt sick. It should be me, not Naoko, accompanying Hanaka.

26

Despite my increasingly desperate attempts to control my universe, two very surprising events occurred in my family over which I had no control. The first related to my brother's bad health during winter, and the second to my father being offered a job.

Johnno had been plagued with bronchitis and asthma and was still, as spring bloomed, quite sickly. The doctor recommended he get some sea air. One afternoon I got home to the news that all of us, Mum, Dad, Johnno and me, were going to Grandma Henderson's for three weeks. Johnno was delighted, as was my mother who, for the first time in ages, seemed light-hearted. Dad was fairly neutral about the expedition, but I was not, as it meant I wouldn't see Hanaka for weeks and weeks because Mum wanted to go as soon as possible but Hanaka was not leaving for Sydney for two more weeks. I pleaded for a stay of another week but the arrangements were all made, Mum said, in what was for her a rather shrill way. With a small shock, I realised that my mother wanted this break desperately. This didn't stop me agitating for what I wanted, also desperately: to keep my presence in Hanaka's life. I pleaded passionately for an extra week, the reason I gave being that I must finish an important project Libby and I were doing together in Geography. Such was my intensity, I think my mother was intimidated and I won my reprieve.

The second surprising event was that on our return from Grandma's, my father would start a new job as a gardener. Once we would have considered this work a come-down but those days were long past. Oldie had arranged the job, apparently through a friend of his, and Dad was to work in the Fitzroy and Treasury Gardens in the city. I learned for the first time that Oldie had something of a name in gardening circles and that he even wrote an advice column for one of the gardening magazines. Oldie told Mum that the work would be really good for Dad and that Oldie's mate would look after him. My mother was very touched.

'He's a truly kind man,' Mum said. 'He had no need to go out of his way to help us, but he did. A lot of people say kind things, but to go that extra distance, to do something practical to help, that's very rare.'

I decided that when next I saw Oldie, I would hug him, but when I rather nervously attempted to, he backed away.

'Don't go all mushy on me, Girlie. Me mate needed a bloke and ya Dad knows how to garden.' But his brown eyes in his funny old wrinkled face seemed to be pleased.

On the Saturday after we got the news about Dad's job we decided to go on an outing to where he'd be working. All of us went, taking the train to Flinders Street Station and then catching a tram up to the edge of the Fitzroy Gardens. Johnno and I had been there once before but he had no memory of it and mine was of bits and pieces like the huge Moreton Bay Fig trees and the model Tudor Village, but little else. Johnno was terribly excited as well as proud as Punch that his father would be able to see these marvels every single day. While I liked the Conservatory and the statue of Diana and the Hounds which stood in the middle of a lily pond outside it, for Johnno it was Captain Cook's cottage that captivated him. He went through the small house at least a dozen times while Dad examined the various plants in the garden beds. Finally we prised Johnno from Cook's cottage with promises of even better thrills: the Fairies Tree and the miniature Tudor Village. The Fairies Tree, the stump of a Red Gum over 300 years old, was carved in 1932 by Ola Cohn with fairies, gnomes, koalas and other animals, and the model Tudor Village was presented to the city of Melbourne in 1948 for our generosity in sending food to England during the War. I hadn't thought of Hanaka all day, but I did then. Imagining how desperately I would miss her, I suddenly missed her in anticipation just as Johnno began pestering me to guess what he liked best out of everything in the Gardens. It was a boring game in which I was supposed to guess all the things he wouldn't like until he decided to tell me. I gave the game short shrift by giving Johnno a sharp, 'What? Tell me.' And Mum said, 'Be patient, Louise.' Johnno proclaimed Captain Cook's cottage to be by far the best because it was older than the Gardens themselves and had been transported from England and rebuilt, brick by brick. My favourite part were the avenues of Elm trees, but Johnno said they didn't count, that it had to be something not in nature, so I said it was the cottage where the Chief Horticulturalist, James Sinclair, had lived. Before he'd come to these gardens and planted the old trees we now saw, he'd assisted Czar Nicholas of Russia in laying out the Royal Gardens in St Petersburg.

'Just imagine,' I said to Johnno, 'If you were one of his children and were allowed to go out into the gardens at night, maybe to chase possums.'

'Or kangaroos,' Johnno said. I looked doubtful.

'Yes, Lou,' he said, 'There'd be lots of kangaroos here in those days. Dingoes too.'

Later, after Dad and Johnno had kicked the footy for a while on a great expanse of lawn, we ate our meat-loaf sandwiches and took turns drinking sweet black tea from the cup of the thermos flask Mum had brought with us. There were even some lemon-iced biscuits for after. On the way home, before catching the train at the station, we walked the short distance to Princes Bridge and stood watching the Yarra River as the bells of St Paul's Cathedral rang out. 'This is my favourite spot in the city,' Dad said. 'Even when I was just a kid, I used to come and stand here looking at the river.' We were all stopped in our tracks by this statement of Dad's because he rarely expressed personal views like this. 'It's mine too, Dad!' said Johnno. Mum and I both agreed it was also a favourite spot of ours. It was a good day for my family.

On waking this morning and before consciousness fully came, I felt the first flutter of butterfly wings across my belly. For the first time I did not believe myself to be in my aunt's house or in my childhood bedroom. For the first time, too, there was no current of sadness for me to push back. Surrounded by large and silent gardens with my husband sleeping beside me, I was aware only of being in my own house, in this city called Melbourne. Suddenly I was so much lighter.

    Exactly how this had come to pass I could not say, but perhaps because my child would be a child of this city, my body had accepted that which my mind and heart resisted.

27

On our last afternoon together before I left for Grandma's, Hanaka and I were eating the biscuits she'd proudly made and reading *The Women's Weekly*. Hanaka's early sickness was gone and she was like spring itself, blooming, her skin lustrous, her joy palpable, bubbling up in laughter and smiles which I sensed rather than knew came from quite another place than one I had any knowledge of. She was a woman holding a wonderful secret, and I couldn't help but watch in fascination.

When we heard a knock on the door, I wanted to say, 'Can't we pretend we're not here?' but what if the person knocking came around the back of the house and saw us? If that thought crossed Hanaka's mind, she ignored it and instead went quickly to answer the door. I heard voices and then an old lady, much older than Grandma, came into the room. It was Mrs Parker, the Quaker lady who Hanaka now called Dorothy. She made herself comfortable, took the cup of tea Hanaka offered and between bites of biscuit told Hanaka some very exciting news. For Hanaka, not for me who wanted the woman gone.

The news was that there was to be a local Rotary Art show and Dorothy, who was on the committee for this event, wanted Hanaka to enter it.

'Yours is such a talent, my dear,' Dorothy told Hanaka. 'You must not keep it to yourself.'

110

Hanaka was so pleased that I forgot my sulk and was pleased too. I still wished Dorothy gone and soon after my wish was granted but not before one heart-stopping moment.

'So, Louise,' Dorothy said. 'Do you live around here?' I answered that I lived a few streets away but I didn't say in which street. I then attempted to steer the conversation to Dorothy's garden, but Dorothy was not easily diverted.

'I've lived here since I married at twenty. Perhaps I know your parents, dear. What surname?'

This caused me to drop my cup and make a loud squealing noise. Did I imagine the rather shrewd look Dorothy gave me?

'Until we meet next time, Louise,' Dorothy said as she took her leave. Which I hoped would never happen.

When Hanaka and I hugged goodbye, she gave me a gift, a small watercolour of how our Japanese garden would look when it was finished: at the edge of the paper was a simple pen drawing of me looking at this garden. I was ecstatic.

'Shall I write on it?' Hanaka asked.

'I know who it's from,' I quickly replied, giving her an almost-bear hug. That way, I wouldn't have to completely hide the drawing away. I could take it to Marlo in the pages of my Geography textbook and if anyone happened to see it, I'd say I found it ... or something ...

❖

Packed and ready to go early next morning, Maggie drove us to Spencer Street Station, from where we'd travel more than one hundred and seventy miles on the train to Bairnsdale and be picked up by Great-Uncle Tom in his 1939 Dodge and driven another seventy odd miles to Grandma's. Uncle Tom only ever drove his Dodge into the nearest big town of Orbost once a week to get groceries and have lunch at the pub with his friends or when something was deemed a very special occasion.

Johnno was particularly excited to be going away but when he'd told Paddy, Paddy bellowed so loudly Mum thought something was seriously wrong. He would not be comforted and kept on repeating a word that sounded like 'telho' which we had no understanding of. By producing not one, but two biscuits, Mum coaxed him to stop crying, and between horrible snotty sniffs we learned that Paddy believed his mother would ship him off to the Tally Ho Boys Home while Johnno was away. Slightly concerned that the over-fecund Mrs O'Shanessy might even do just that, Mum walked Paddy home, but it turned out that only when Paddy got too much for her did she threaten to ring up the Home. 'He can be a right little bastard,' Mrs O'Shanessy explained to my suitably horrified mother. From that day onwards, Paddy never had to ask for a biscuit.

I'd already given Oldie the agreed-on payment to dig Hanaka's garden and he was going to do the job at the beginning of the second week she'd be away. I also now possessed the coveted ruby shoes which I kept in a space below the bottom drawer of my dressing table. Although my hiding place would be really hard to find, I still didn't put it past Maggie to have a good snoop around while we were gone so I'd asked Libby to take the shoes for safekeeping while I was away. She was having some problems at home too, something with her father that she wouldn't talk about, and she was more than happy to assist any teenage rebellion. As I could only wear the shoes away from my home, I was faced with a number of strategic difficulties whenever I wanted to wear them which, so far, I'd only done once. Had I really understood that because of the manner of getting the ruby shoes, I would only ever be able to wear them secretly?

Of course, if I wanted shoes my family couldn't afford and stole in order to have them, I must then keep both the stealing and the shoes a secret: I understood that but, occasionally, doubts assailed me. Why did I go to such an extreme as stealing to possess something which then could only be worn clandestinely? Although I'd *almost* convinced myself I was doing no real harm by stealing Maggie's money, I hadn't told Libby, nor had I told her the truth about my father's illness being of the mental kind, rather than, as she believed, a physical illness because of the war. More crucially, why was one of the most important people in my life, Hanaka, totally unknown to my family? These questions confused me greatly but I was unable to take any action that might rectify the situation because ... because ... I didn't know why.

On our way to Grandma's we passed countryside green from recent rain, the air carrying the faint scent of the eucalypts edging the road. Crossing the Snowy River before Orbost then following the road along the river, fields of maize and maize barns on one side, dark-reddish mahogany gums on the river side and, across the river, the jagged hills known as the Devil's Backbone, we searched for the familiar landmark which would tell us we were almost there. 'I see them!' said Mum, pointing to the tips of sand dunes in the distance which separate the Snowy from the sea. I'd never seen her so excited. Then we were crossing the Brodribb River which runs into the Snowy, up the hill, and finally we arrived at Grandma's!

28

Nature was showing off in the small hamlet of Marlo where Grandma lived. While much of the vegetation surrounding the town was scrubby bush, the gardens of houses, many holiday homes for people from the district, were planted with camellias, hydrangeas, lilies and roses as well as natives. Local wisdom was that it was hard to kill a plant in Marlo, the soil being perfect and the heavy rainfall keeping everything green except during the hot summer months. Also, it was generally acknowledged that the sunsets of Marlo were one of the wonders of the world. As were the size of the mosquitoes.

Grandma had afternoon tea ready for us, scones and jam and cream and ginger cake and we ravenously tucked in. Uncle Tom hadn't said much, in fact, 'Good to see youse' were the only words he'd spoken so far, but that was his way. When his wife Esme was alive they rarely spoke to one another which was, as Grandma said, 'Usually a sure sign the marriage was bad.' But Tom and Esme were the exception: 'I've never seen a more devoted couple. No need for words: they each knew what the other was thinking.'

Aunt Esme had died of a stroke five years ago while she was in the milking shed. Uncle Tom carried on, but we all knew his heart was broken. 'Can it get fixed?' Johnno asked recently when Mum had said this, his face all screwed up. 'We hope so,' Mum said brightly. 'If it was his leg, and not his heart,' I put in, 'It would get better but not completely.'

'You mean Uncle Tom will always have a limp in his heart?'

We agreed that this was so.

For the first week, every morning after breakfast, Johnno and I walked beside the Snowy River to its entrance to the ocean. When the tide was out, you could swim and wade across to the sand and the ocean, but it was still too cold to do that yet, and anyhow, Johnno wasn't allowed until he could swim. I'd promised to teach him during the next summer. On our first walk we'd taken Foolish, Grandma's dog, but after about ten minutes he'd sat down and refused to move, so we had to carry him back to the house. Foolish was old, fifteen, blind in one eye and had the rheumatism, Grandma said. He was one of two brothers, the other named Clever but as Grandma said, not so clever he didn't manage to get himself killed by a truck. We often passed fishermen on our walks, sometimes in groups of two or three but sometimes alone. Johnno never felt the need to whisper, 'Ho, ho, jelly-bean' to these lone men because he knew what they were up to. If the fish were biting, a crowd of eager pelicans would gather for the waste from the cleaned bream or whiting or the many other fish which lived in the river. On mornings when no humans were about and the river was tranquil, we often saw black swans as well as cormorants diving for food then surfacing a surprising distance away. Johnno and I played a game where we'd each guess how long before the cormorant would emerge, using slow counting as our clock, with the winner being whoever guessed the closest time.

One morning Johnno wanted to go to Uncle Tom's with Dad, so I went walking by myself. The differing moods of the river enchanted me and that morning the bright sunlight made it seem as though there were a thousand candles just beneath its slightly choppy surface. A short distance ahead a lone heron stood completely still. It was not usual to see a heron on this part of the river as they are wary of people and preferred further down the river in a place called Frenchs Narrows. Herons had gained new meaning for me because Hanaka had told me the folk tale of the heron saved by a woodcutter which, in reward, turns into a beautiful woman and becomes the man's wife. To help the woodcutter earn money, the Heron Maiden transforms back into a heron and weaves a magnificent cape from her own feathers. Again and again she does this despite the pain it causes her until finally the woodcutter, seeing her lying bleeding, understands what he has asked of her. Deeply ashamed, and for love of her, the woodcutter returns the Heron Maiden to the wild.

Wondering how near I could get without the heron flying away, I moved slowly and quietly until I was close enough to see that its eyes were closed. Suddenly, catching a slight movement, the bird made a strange cry and flew to the centre of the river. Rather than flying over to the ocean side of the river, instead the heron flew straight down the centre of the river and landed again not so very far from me. For the next few mornings I saw the heron in almost the same place but every time I'd *almost* get as close as I'd dare to, she flew away. In a whimsy, I declared the bird to be the Heron Maiden.

Although I missed Hanaka, truth to tell, I didn't miss her as much as I'd believed I would. Before I went to sleep most nights I'd look at her garden painting but sometimes I'd forget because every day was such a whirl of activity and people coming and going. Dad helped Uncle Tom most days with the milking or fixing fences and machinery. He and Tom seemed to be able to work side by side with hardly a word between them, though Dad said you could get Tom going if you asked him to tell you stories about the Snowy River floods. The Snowy flooded frequently and only two years before had flooded a total of seven times! Each flood meant loss of stock, ruin of maize and bean crops, houses too, with mud in everything as well as the stink of it drying for weeks later. But Uncle Tom always wound up another flood story with his oft-repeated opinion that these floods made the river flats 'as fertile as the Nile delta in Egypt'. He was good on the history too. In the old days before the roads were made and the railway came as far as Orbost, all goods and people arrived from Melbourne and Lakes Entrance at the Port of Marlo in schooners, steamers and other vessels. Barges were then filled up with the goods these ships carried, such as machinery parts, bales of wool, sacks of salt and bricks, and towed up the Snowy River to Orbost by the paddle steamer *The Curlip*. On the return journey the barges carried maize and other produce to be taken as far away as Melbourne. Because the roads were so bad, the doctor for the district often had to travel by horseback to see his patients. The old hotel at Marlo used to be where well-off people stayed for holidays to enjoy fishing, boating and picnics. At one stage the hotel even had a bowling green and a tennis court for the guests' amusement. The hotel was still here, although changed somewhat, and with neither bowling green nor tennis court.

Sometimes Uncle Tom and Dad went out fishing in the tinny and a couple of times came back with ten or twelve fish. Johnno went once but after the initial excitement he was restless and worried that the boat might sink. I liked going out on the river but although I was happy to eat the fish I didn't much enjoy seeing them wriggling on the hook. Apart from the river, my favourite place was the dairy. I loved everything about it: herding the cows into the milking stalls with the help of Tosser, Uncle Tom's dog, the smell of cow-dung, the creamy-white milk flowing into buckets which was later put into big drums and left for the milk truck. Uncle Tom had a bloke called Davo who helped him with the milking. I'd learned to milk too, but not very well and sometimes my cow would put her foot in the bucket and ruin the milk. Uncle Tom brought a bucket of milk to Grandma's every day and, after letting it settle, she'd take the cream off the top and use the rest for cooking and drinking. Grandma and Mum seemed to spend most of their time in the sunny kitchen which overlooked the river estuary, sandhills and the sea. They chattered together as they cooked, and this cooking and its results had a vitality

117

sadly lacking in our own home; perhaps it was because my mother had Grandma for company as well as the fact that Grandma considered cooking to be a very serious art. Mum and Grandma were also sewing new curtains for both Aunt Lily's house and for ours, as well as cutting out patterns for two new summer dresses for Mum. Uncle Tom called them 'the whirling dervishes' which thrilled Johnno no end, even more so when he was told that the name was for a group of Middle Eastern mystics who whipped themselves into a state by whirling. He tried it but made himself sick.

Aunt Lily came over for tea sometimes but then she had to be taken home and helped into bed. She didn't say much but her sharp brown eyes never missed a trick. She often asked for more pudding and sometimes said mysterious things such as 'It was definitely spotted but the tea-cosy was mine.' That certainly kept us guessing! Another time she said to Johnno in a very fierce way, 'So you're poor Molly's boy ... better be good or she'll put you in the chook shed.' Forget poor Molly's boy, whoever he was, poor Johnno was quite frightened!

After tea and the washing-up we usually read – Johnno was halfway through *A Little Bush Maid*, the first book in the *Billabong* series by Mary Grant Bruce which had been Mum's, but it was a bit too hard for him so he and Mum or he and I read some together each night. I was reading *The Woman in White* and loving it, Mum was deep into *Come in Spinner* and Dad, *The Great Houdini*, all out of the Library Man's battered suitcases. Grandma was reading her knitting pattern book. We read by the light of gas lamps because Marlo didn't yet have the electricity connected. When I was little we had kerosene lamps, which were awfully smelly. Grandma showed us photos of Mum when she was a baby and at other stages of growing up, as well as both herself and Grandpa too. Grandma looked really young in the photos because she was only nineteen when Mum was born. Grandpa had been killed in a logging accident when Mum was ten. 'Grandma never considered getting married again,' Mum told me once, 'even though she had many would-be suitors.' Some nights we played Monopoly but after Grandma taught us to play poker that became our game. We played for matches because Grandma had made Johnno and me promise that we'd never gamble for money.

During the day friends and neighbours dropped in for a cuppa and invited Mum and Grandma, and me too if I wanted, to afternoon tea or a flower show or to someone's birthday party. Mum visited girls she'd known from school who would then ask her to come to an amateur theatrical production or a Red Cross do. Our whole family went to the Golden Wedding Anniversary of a friend of Grandma's and Uncle Tom's, and as the toast to the couple was called and everyone raised their glasses, a thin fierce old woman called out, 'Up with temperance!' It must have been a regular occurrence as nobody paid her any attention at all except my wide-eyed family: the men continued drinking their beers while the ladies sipped sherries or shandies. But the really spectacular event was that my father who I'd never heard sing in all of my life, even though I'd been told that once upon a time, before he went to war, he'd had a wonderful voice, was persuaded to sing. He sang old songs, *There'll be Bluebirds Over the White Cliffs of Dover* and then, *Comin' Through the Rye* and then, along with us all, *Auld Lang Syne.* He sang in a way that made me glad he was my father and, as he sang, Johnno's eyes never moved from my father's face. Then someone called out, 'What about us Irish? Sing *Danny Boy!*' Mum almost froze in horror making me remember that there was a secret about a Danny which might be the cause of my father's war neurosis. Quickly, Mum whispered something to Grandma who clapped her hands and said loudly, 'Let's hear from Alf and his fiddle!' and the moment when things could so easily have gone bad passed, leaving us only with the memory of my father's lovely voice.

The following weeks slipped from one delightful day into the next and the next. Grandma chattered and bustled all day, my mother too, even though I'd never thought of her as the bustling type. I'd never seen my mother so energised and

119

my father too, in his own way. He'd put on weight as well as some muscle and seemed so much more ... what? Here. That was it – Dad was *here* with us in the present. Even when he and Uncle Tom sat silently companionable on the verandah after the afternoon milking was done, with Foolish and Tosser asleep at their feet, my father was *here*. It was a minor miracle and I had no doubt it was due to Grandma Henderson. We had all drawn vigour from her, not just her bustling but her mental energy and connection with the life around her.

On our last morning I woke early, crept out of the sleeping house and down to the river. The river was at low tide, a pearly blue-grey and, above, the high swirling clouds were tinged with shades of pink. Three pelicans glided in the soft wind. The *Heron Maiden* stood motionless but as I purposely ran toward her, blowing kisses, she flew into the centre of the river and then, as I called, 'goodbye, goodbye', she let out a harsh croaking cry and with wings beating almost languidly, long legs trailing, flew over to the other side.

29

Buoyed by our holiday and its successes, we returned home a more confident family than the one who'd set out. Johnno's health had improved a great deal and he hardly coughed or wheezed and, perhaps even better, his funny little pinched expression so familiar to us was largely gone. Mum looked years younger and she often *laughed.* Not so long ago she would have had difficulty finding something to laugh at. Dad too looked younger and I could now recognise him as the man in the silver frame. As for me, I'd enjoyed myself immensely with my family and, although I was looking forward to seeing Hanaka again, I'd been less miserable than I'd believed I would be. Far less. Maybe not miserable at all. Perversely, that had helped me feel confident – that word again – about our friendship. Confidence, self-assurance: such words were always a bad fit with my family but now they'd become possibilities.

For myself, being away from the scene of the crime so to speak, had given me distance to examine my own behaviour. What frightened me more than my moral lack in stealing from Maggie was the reckless way I'd gone about it. It was as if another girl, a *wild, rash, egotistical* girl, had committed these crimes. That wasn't the kind of girl I wanted to be. I wanted to be a heroine! Not a goody-goody but one who was brave and whose sometimes daring acts only ever resulted in excellent consequences: I wanted to be honourable. Squirming in shame at the thought of being caught, of my mother and father knowing what I'd done, of Johnno knowing, I resolved never to steal again. I would get an after-school job and buy what I needed with the money I'd earn. Despite this soul-searching, I never questioned my friendship with Hanaka: it was fixed and I would not chance it by being open with my family. Hanaka had spoken about karma which was part of Buddhist belief and was like something being predestined. That's how I viewed my relationship with her.

We arrived at the station expecting Maggie to pick us up, but she was nowhere in sight.

'Perhaps she didn't get my letter,' Mum said, 'but I posted it 12 days ago.'

'Bloody Maggie,' said Dad.

There was nothing to do but pick up our suitcases, get back on another train then a tram, tired and hungry to boot. Johnno ran ahead of us down the street to home. None of us had his energy nor his suitcase-less state but we were more than glad to see home too. The birds twittered in the late afternoon as they began nestling into the palm at the front. Home! There's no place like ... Mum opened the front door. She stopped and sniffed. Was she turning into a sniffer like Grandma? We soon found out why. The air was more than stale, it reeked of cigarettes and something else. 'Grog,' Dad said. But the smell was more than just grog. The lounge-room was littered with cups, glasses, bottles, clothes, overflowing ashtrays, old crusts and bits of dried food on plates.

'It's a pig-sty!' Mum was aghast and more so when we reached the kitchen. Burnt sausages in congealed fat stuck to the frying pan and dirty dishes, some with food in various states of decomposition on them, were piled up on every surface. Stinking garbage spilled from the Inside Bin having never been deposited into the Outside Bin in the whole time we were away. Milk bottles half-full of milk, some with mould on the top, were on the sink. At his first glance of the kitchen Johnno had taken off, probably to check that his bower had not been touched. Mum began searching the cupboards for something to eat.

'What the hell's been going on here?' Dad asked. We were all discombobulated, my new favourite word, but I didn't like what it felt like. Then Johnno was back, tugging at my jumper. 'Lou ... Lou ... she's in there ...' he whispered. 'Asleep.' And she was. Apparently. I didn't get to see her as Mum told us to go and buy fish and chips for tea as well as milk and bread if there were any to be got at this late time of day. Johnno put into words what had been welling up inside me from the moment I'd stepped inside my home.

'I thought everything would be alright, Lou ... But it's not, is it?' His face was once again pinched with anxiety.

'It will be,' I told him. 'I promise, Johnno.' Ah, promises! Not to mention self-assurance and confidence which in the time it takes to open a front door lock can bloom, unlike a caterpillar to a gorgeous butterfly, into anxiety and dread.

'Aunt Maggie's room smelt ... like sick,' Johnno said.

Sick and smelly and dirty and drunk. That's what Mum whispered to me when we returned home with the fish and chips. We told Johnno that Maggie had the flu.

'She shouldn't drink grog when she's got the flu,' he said. We agreed this was so.

'Maggie won't be drinking any more,' Mum's voice contained a chunk of ice.

We were all ravenous and the fish and chips which were a treat even in these circumstances were finished in a flash. Then we set to clean up the mess, Johnno to pick up all dirty cups and glasses from the lounge room and me to tackle the kitchen with Dad while Mum went to tackle Maggie.

'Don't come out,' she ordered us all. 'Leave her to me.'

Mum came back into the kitchen about half an hour later carrying a bundle of bed linen and other clothes which she carried through to the wash-house. She did not look impressed.

'You'll have to talk to her, Jack,' she said when she came back. 'Not now – she's in the bath with a terrible head. Tomorrow when she's herself again.'

'What can I do?' asked Dad.

'You can tell her she has to stop! Or else go and live somewhere else! Because I'm not living with your sister if she drinks like this.'

Dad sat down suddenly as if everything was too much for him. I too wished I was somewhere far, far from here – or even a few streets away, safe from all this with Hanaka.

30

When Hanaka opened her back door to me I almost fainted! No longer a small, willowy woman but an obviously pregnant one, she'd bloomed as if a thousand peonies resided within her – I'm being fanciful – but her blooming indeed seemed synonymous with a garden richly embroidered by the imagination.

'I am so pleased to see you, Louise,' she said, giving me a hug. I was in heaven as we walked to the lounge room.

'This is my friend, Naoko, whom I visited Sydney with,' Hanaka said, indicating a rather plump woman smiling at me from the couch.

Go away! I didn't say that, but I wanted to. Naoko didn't say much but smiled and nodded agreeably as Hanaka talked. Occasionally Hanaka translated something into Japanese and a short conversation would follow between the two of them. When Naoko got up to leave she said goodbye to me with a small bow after which she and Hanaka had a lengthy conversation. I realised that I'd never before heard Hanaka speak her own language. As I watched them from the window they bowed to each other. It was like being transported for a moment into another world. When Hanaka came back inside she told me that her friend Chie had sent her three Japanese books as well as two teacups and some green tea. Would I like to try it? Although the green tea was not unpleasant it was most strange, but the teacups we drank from made up for any disappointment with the taste. The two cups, one slightly larger than the other, were decorated with leaves and magenta camellias outlined with gold-leaf. The Japanese certainly loved their camellias! I drank more green tea than I really wanted because of the pleasure using the teacup gave me.

As we sipped, Hanaka told me that Naoko's English was not very good, and how hard that was for her.

'She's nice,' I said even as I wished her a million miles away from Hanaka.

'Naoko is a kind person,' Hanaka replied. 'Her life is very difficult.'

'She seems happy,' I said.

'Naoko smiles to make others comfortable,' Hanaka said. 'A Japanese woman will never show her private grief.'

'What grief?' I asked.

'Her husband already has children ... his wife before, died. He will not give Naoko a child because ... because he does not want a child who is ... half and half ...'

'Poor Naoko.' I was intrigued how Naoko's husband made sure he never gave her a child. If he could do that, couldn't anyone? I wanted someone to tell me.

'But what about if ... there's a "mistake"?' Paddy had told us gleefully that he was a 'mistake' as were his sister Grace and baby brother Brian. On that occasion Mum gave him two biscuits.

'A mistake?' Hanaka was puzzled. Perhaps she didn't know anything either.

'You know ... you don't want a baby but then you *are* having a baby...'

'Ah! Mistake!' Hanaka laughed but then very seriously said, 'Naoko's husband will not allow any mistake.'

What was Naoko's husband's secret? Did he ... *never* ... with Naoko? Or was there some other way? Like Mum had hinted? And if there was, why did so many young couples like Libby's brother Pete who was only nineteen, still have a 'shotgun' wedding because his girlfriend, Annette, was having a big 'mistake'?

126

What did Hanaka think about this half and half business, because that's what her own baby would be? Before I'd thought, I blurted out, 'He shouldn't have married her then, should he? If he was so worried about a baby being ... you know ... not accepted ...'

Hanaka's face became a mask, which I knew meant she was upset. Pregnant women weren't supposed to get upset! I quickly changed the subject to Oldie's digging and we went outside to inspect his handiwork. Oldie had done a thorough job – every bit of earth was completely turned over and the clods broken up. As well, the azaleas and camellia bush had been expertly pruned. This is what I'd wanted, wasn't it? But what to do now? I had no idea. Fortunately Hanaka did.

'We'll need to put some plants in here,' she said, pointing, 'More azaleas, but most important is to make the path. Alan is getting some wood for that.'

'What about stones for the path?' I asked.

'Wood is easier to get, and his friend can get it for nothing – it will be quite expensive for us to buy the plants and what else is needed.'

I hadn't thought of that.

'I can get some cuttings from my garden,' I said. I'd heard Oldie and my father use that word, but I really didn't understand how it worked. Did you simply break off a piece of a plant and stick it in the ground and it grew? I knew you could do that with geraniums, but what of other plants?

'We will plant the maple tree right here,' Hanaka said.

'Yes! Then we can plant the rest of the garden around it.'

'I wish we could plant the tree now – it is the best time – but Dorothy says maples of a good size are expensive so we may have to wait, even to the autumn.'

'How expensive?' I asked.

'I think, for a good tree, maybe £4 ... even more ...' We were both silent for a moment.

'Is your friend knowledgeable about plants?' Hanaka asked.

127

For a moment I didn't know who she was talking about.

'Perhaps he could come and advise us.' She meant Oldie!

'Er ... he doesn't know much about plants at all ... only good for chopping and digging really ...'

'The way he has pruned the camellia bush is very professional looking.'

That's when I changed the subject to the Sydney Harbour Bridge.

Later, while Mum and I did the dishes, I asked, 'When two people of different races, say a Chinese and an Australian marry and have a baby...What do you think ...?'

'It's hard for the children, isn't it?' Mum said. 'I always feel sorry for them because they're neither one thing nor the other.

'Why?' I didn't understand why it should be so hard. I didn't want it to be hard for Hanaka's baby.

'Oh, Louise, I don't know, I suppose people want to preserve their own race and its customs and each think their own better than the other – so when there's mixed race children well, that throws a spanner in the works.'

'Because the man and woman have broken the rules? But they're not real rules.'

'It's human nature to stick to your own kind.'

'So if I had a baby with a man from China you wouldn't want to be the grandmother?'

'Don't be silly. Of course. But stop talking rubbish. How many Chinese men have you met lately?'

'Mr Lim!' We both laughed.

'Mr Lim's a good illustration – his great-grandfather came to Australia about the same time as our ancestors. Mr Lim married a Chinese woman and his son, Robert, did too. His grand-daughter's about twenty now. She'll most likely marry a Chinese boy.'

'She's an Australian. Maybe she'll marry an Australian like us.'

128

'The Chinese stick to their own, just like we do,' Mum said. 'It's for the best.'

How could it be for the best if it meant a little child who was half one race and half another like Hanaka's baby would be, was made to feel that she didn't belong? It just wasn't fair!

'Look what happened when one race believed it was much better than all other races!'

'What?'

'Mum! The Nazis!'

'That was extreme.'

'But it happened! It can't be a good thing, Mum, to have people believing that they're better than someone else because they're ... Do you think you're better than Mr Lim?'

Mum was slightly wrong-footed by my question and mumbled, 'No. But would it really be better if we were all mixed up?'

Clearly she didn't think so. Who had made these rules, I wondered.

I had never seen a mixed-race child around my neighbourhood and the only Asians I knew were Mr Lim and his family, and now Hanaka. I knew that some Chinese people lived in the city and once Libby's neighbours, who were 'bohemians', had a really black man come and stay at their house. Libby was thrilled. He was from America she said and was a professor of something and so nice. Then I remembered Annie who helped Grandma in Aunt Lily's house.

'What about Annie? Grandma's Annie?'

'Ah, Annie,' Mum said. 'Yes, that was very sad.'

Annie with the pale golden skin and cornflower-blue eyes had been taken away from her mother by the Government when she was four years old. She was put in a home in another State, her mother not knowing where she was. But somehow, some people tracked her down and, when she turned sixteen, Annie was reunited with her Aboriginal family in East Gippsland. I asked Mum why she'd been taken away.

'The Authorities thought it was for the best,' Mum said.

129

'Why?'

'I think they wanted her to be able to grow up to be white.'

'But that's cruel! How would you like it if Johnno was taken away and you didn't know where he was or if you'd ever see him again?'

'It ... oh, I don't know, Louise ... It was supposed to be best for the child ... '

What if, say, Alan died and the government decided it was for the best to take Hanaka's half and half baby away from her? How could that ever be for the best? Maybe one day it might even be *interesting* to have two people from different races for your parents; maybe, instead of not belonging to either world or in danger of being taken away, maybe you might be lucky and belong in both worlds.

When we first became lovers and knew we never wanted to part, Alan said to me, 'It'll be hard, Hanaka. Not only for us, but for our children.' I did not want to hear this and protested that a child of our union would be much better off in Australia where we would always be able to protect her, than in Japan. Most people here are kind, but not all ... and it is true I belong to a race that was an enemy of the Australian people. My husband's sister-in-law hates me because of that and the Chinese vegetable seller also because of the terrible actions of the Imperial Army in China. In Sydney a man spat when Naoko and I walked by. All this I can bear. But for that hatred to be passed on to my child I could not bear.

It is amusing to think of my naivety in the cooking classes before I came to Australia. It is terrifying to think of my naivety regarding a child who is a half and half. Louise was right when she said that Naoko's husband should not have married her nor brought her far from her home if he never intended to have a child with her. He has always seemed to me a man who has some kind of darkness within. Perhaps his

130

darkness is that he can see no hope for a future that allows kindness and acceptance to be stronger than hatred.

Alan too worries about our child but he only tells me his hopeful thoughts, not his fears. 'Australia's changing, Hanaka,' he said last night. 'So many people are coming here from all parts of the world. Soon it will become a place where it's easier to be different.'

Tonight I will join Dorothy and the Friends and sit silently in expectant waiting for these 'divine leadings'. Sometimes, many people have this happen and they speak and other times we sit silently for the hour. At the end of each Meeting we shake hands with each other. Although I do not entirely understand this Quakerism, I find much comfort at these Meetings where I am neither intimidated by expectations nor feel myself one apart. Yet it is still true that if I were in my homeland I would go to a temple with an offering of oranges for Kannon and ask her to grant my prayer that my child will grow up wanted and loved by her country.

31

Unlike Naoko who hid her true feelings so others would not be made uncomfortable, Maggie felt free to lament loudly and at length at how the world had done her wrong. All the rest of us, except Johnno, had a hard time holding in our feelings of impatience and annoyance at her self-pity. Johnno told me that Maggie was unhappy and I should try to make her feel better. I didn't think it right to tell him that the only way I could ever succeed in making Maggie feel better was by breaking both legs and catching polio. I stayed out of Maggie's way and helped Mum as much as I could because she was the one who bore the brunt of it. Mum and I decided it was best if we didn't burden Dad about Maggie as any stress upset him badly and he was only just getting over the state that Maggie and the house had been in on our return. He'd started his gardening job and we all tried to take a great interest in his day's doings. On his first day, when he came home in the late afternoon Johnno made a big fuss of him, getting him a cup of tea and his slippers.

Mum felt sorry for Maggie but such was Maggie's nature that she was a difficult and bad-tempered unhappy person alternately whingeing to Mum or crying and wanting to be comforted. Apparently she'd gone to work drunk and sworn at her boss and would have got the sack but for her connections with the Union and in particular, Bill, who'd used his influence to spare Maggie; instead her punishment was a demotion. Now Maggie would have to work in a draughty ticket office rather than the more congenial and better-paid place she'd worked in since before the war ended. She'd been given a month's leave on doctor's orders but, with two weeks of it already gone, we didn't see her being fit enough to go back to work in another two weeks. Part of this was due to the re-emergence of Bill in her life, albeit briefly and only in order to help her out. He was, Maggie told Mum, a sad, sad man because his daughter had died two months before. Mum said Maggie still believed that if he came back to her, she could make the sadness go. But Bill was living with his wife and two other children and his helping hand to Maggie was just that.

'Perhaps he felt guilty,' Mum said. 'She really did love him. Still does.' Poor Bill. I might have even said poor Maggie except I'd learned from experience that as soon as I'd ever had sympathy for her, Maggie would go and do or say something horrible.

One afternoon when I'd come straight home from school rather than going to Hanaka's, and was feeling just a little put out because she was spending the day with Naoko, Oldie was working in our garden.

'So Girlie, what did your friend think?' I was a blank.

'The garden I dug! I thought I might have done it wrong. I was thinkin' of goin' round to ask.'

Suddenly I was very alert. 'They loved it! I forgot to tell you! Sorry, Oldie. They were very pleased.'

'So what sort of garden is it goin' to be?'

'Um ... azaleas and um ... I'm not sure ...'

'Azaleas ... Japanese ...Ya know when we talked about those plants from there? Ya gone dumb or somethin'? You remember, Girlie?'

I didn't want to be having this conversation at all. 'I remember ... but I've got to go, Oldie ... lots of homework.'

'Ha! Homework can always wait. I've got something real interestin' to tell ya. I went into the library, the big bugger in town, and found out that these European botanist blokes first collected specimens of Japanese plants in the 1700s. It

133

was really hard because the Shogun wouldn't let hardly any Europeans in because he was afraid they'd try to convert the Japs to Christianity, or somethin' like that, and so ya had to get permission to travel anywhere and mind your Ps and Qs or ya'd lose ya head pretty quick smart. There was one Russian bloke who introduced hydrangeas to Russia. How about that! Interestin'?'

It was: the history of plants was tied up with the history of people in a way I'd never thought of before. I simply couldn't resist. 'Did you read anything about maple trees?' I asked.

'Maples? As a matter of fact I did ... let me see if I can remember it right. One bloke, later, in the 1800s – Von Siebold – sent back a lot of plants and introduced them into gardens in Europe. The Botanic Garden in Lieden – that's in Holland – got hold of some, and a few, includin' a maple, are still alive today. We could actually go and see it, Girlie. I reckon that's pretty bloody good.'

I did too, but what would be even better would be to find a mature maple tree here in Melbourne which cost only about five shillings!

'We've got azaleas, haven't we?'

'Yeah ... look ... there ... and over there and in the back. They grow from cuttings ... ya could give a few to ya friends ...'

I would've liked to ask Oldie to take some cuttings but I knew to do so would further risk the whole secret of Hanaka. As it was, if I didn't watch it, Oldie would be around at Hanaka's having a morning cuppa.

'They've got tons of plants from relatives,' I told him, picking up my school bag to go into the house. Just before I disappeared inside Oldie called out, 'How's that broken leg?' What broken leg?

'Ya friend's hubby. How's his leg goin?'

I wasn't sorry I'd asked Oldie to dig the garden because otherwise I doubted it would've ever been done, but now I wanted him to show absolutely no more interest in it!

134

Although it was true that the Maggie mess had given our confidence a good slap in the face, we'd recovered surprisingly quickly. It seemed that each one of us now had a different outlook, one more in keeping with what I called the 'Marlo Philosophy' that Grandma and Uncle Tom, and the place itself, had passed on to us. This Marlo Philosophy was about being able to imagine, then determinedly work toward, a different possibility. Mum in particular seemed to have gained strength from the time she'd spent in her girlhood home and there was a new kind of resolve evident in her. When she went off to hear the Reverend Light give his sermon every Sunday maybe that resolve was reinforced. However it had happened, I liked it. With Mum more in control of what happened or how she reacted to what happened, I felt some of my old anxieties slipping into the back seat of my brain.

Mum never talked much about the meaning of her church-going but it was evident that it was now an important part of her life. She'd volunteered to do the church flowers once a month, a job not as easy as it sounded because of the rivalry between different ladies regarding how the Rev liked the flowers to be. Mum thought this quite touching. 'Poor things,' she said of these bickering women. 'Reverend Light couldn't care less about the flowers but they fight over them because they're all in love with him.'

'He's old! They are too!'

'You can still fall in love when you're old, Louise.'

No! Have those glorious fluttery feelings in your chest and in 'the nether regions' as Grandma called them when she urged Johnno not to forget to wash there when he was in the bath? Like I did with Toluk? Like I did when I pressed my legs tightly together? Like Maria and Robert *plainly* did in *For Whom the Bell Tolls*? No! I certainly hoped I'd never feel like that when I was old!

One of the best things we'd brought home from Grandma's was Dad's once lost voice. This was largely to do with Johnno who, enthralled by his father's singing at the anniversary party, became almost obsessed with making sure Dad didn't tumble down again into silence. Johnno began listening to popular songs on the radio and trying to learn the words off by heart. This proved hilariously difficult – our first version of *Mambo Italiano* was not quite as the songwriter had intended – but as Johnno couldn't write the words down, both because he wasn't fast enough and his spelling wasn't up to it, I was roped in to listen and write down the words of the songs. Thus I came to know all the words to *Hernandez Hideaway*, *Papa loves Mambo* and *I Can't Tell a Waltz from a Tango*. None of us knew much about Mambos or Tangos or places like Hernandez Hideaway but we loved these songs full of rhythm and fun.

One night, after the dishes were all washed and put away and I'd done my homework, or most of it, and Johnno had done his reading from the third grade reader, we got ready for our singalong. Dad was particularly tired and Mum told Johnno that we should leave it but Dad said no, he wanted to sing but not for more than half an hour. We always started with the mambo-tangos and then songs from the radio.

Maggie was due to start work again in a week's time and all of us, particularly Mum who was stuck with her all day, couldn't wait for that to happen. Suffering was supposed to make you a better person and although I wasn't sympathetic to Maggie, I knew she'd suffered, but now she acted like a woman born sucking lemons. We'd been singing a particularly crazy version of *Papa loves Mambo*. Johnno had 'the mads' as Mum called them, and was jumping around like a two bob watch when we saw Maggie leaning against the doorway.

'The happy family,' she said, her voice a sneer.

136

We fell silent, except for Johnno, hopeful little Johnno. 'Aunt Maggie. It's such fun. Come and sing with us.'

'Ha! You're nothing but a little freak.' Johnno looked as if he'd been slapped. Dad began to get out of his chair, his hands visibly shaking. As for me, I wanted to throttle her until she was dead. But it was Mum who stood up and said. 'That is unforgiveable Maggie. Unforgiveable. I will not have you speaking to Johnno like that.'

'What are you going to do about it?' Maggie turned on her heel and marched back to her room.

Mum spent the rest of the evening soothing Johnno and Dad. She knew I would never be soothed. What Mum didn't know was that I was going to make Maggie pay. Literally. What I didn't know was that Maggie had crossed the Rubicon as far as my mother was concerned and she *really* was going to do something about it.

That night, I awoke to the sounds of my father's screams. After the first rush of terror, I knew it was his old nightmare. Did I imagine I heard him call 'Danny'? Or was it that I knew his nightmare was about Danny? I leapt out of bed but stopped when I heard Mum's voice soothing him. Johnno, mercifully, slept on, but not Maggie, who was standing in the hall. 'It's all your fault,' I hissed.

32

I practically sprinted to Hanaka's a few afternoons later, anxious to report my dramatic day. On the way to school that morning, Libby told me she was going to live with her grandparents. She began to cry even before she got the words out and then I, like an idiot, started crying too and then we both began to laugh like loons. The real shock for me was that Libby was leaving school. Her grandparents wanted her to go to a private girls' school, which was closer to their house. I knew Libby had fights with her father, but to leave home? I couldn't understand it. I'd envied her family's beach house and Libby's bedroom, wall-papered with sprigs of roses, the new bikes and the most-up-to-date gramophone and records as well as *two* telephones, but most of all I'd envied her happy family. Something really terrible must have happened. All day Libby and I stuck to one another like leeches, crying mainly during recess times but during class Libby couldn't always hold the tears back. The other kids mostly kept out of our way but a couple of boys came and tentatively patted Libby on the shoulder before offering us both sweets. We took them, but didn't stop crying. Miss Blyth, the sewing teacher, wanted to know what was wrong and I said that Libby's aunt had died.

'Why are you crying too, Louise?' she asked.

'In sympathy,' I replied.

'If you must cry, do so quietly.' Miss Blyth was a Scottish woman whose principal personality attribute might be described as dourness, a word Grandma used to describe some of our Scottish forebears.

When I got to Hanaka's on that spring afternoon, full to bursting with Libby's drama, Hanaka was sitting in the sun-room where we always liked to sit. I could see her through the window, but although she looked up at my approach, she didn't greet me with her usual smile nor did she get up from her chair. The wire back door was un-snibbed and I went straight in, my heart racing not from running but in fear of what I thought I could see on Hanaka's face.

'The baby?' I asked.

'She is safe here,' Hanaka said, indicating her small bulge.

I sat down next to her. 'What's wrong then?'

Hanaka smiled gently but, oh, it was a smile to truly break a heart.

'Tell me ...'

'I am always trying very hard ...'

'Who came today? Mother McDonald ...?'

Hanaka didn't reply but turned her head as she pressed her hands to her eyes. I got up and went into the kitchen to make us both tea and when I came back Hanaka was in exactly the same position. I gave her the tea and she held it but didn't drink.

'Was she unkind?' I asked.

'It is too hard,' Hanaka whispered. Alarmed by something in her voice I took the tea cup from her and held her hand in mine.

'Mother McDonald shouldn't be nasty to you. You have to tell Alan.'

'I cannot.'

'Hanaka. You must. It isn't right for her to treat you like this!'

'She is Alan's mother. I must be stronger.' That was it. Hanaka was all out of fight. It frightened me.

'Please Hanaka ... tell him ... he'll understand.' I searched my mind for words that would make Hanaka believe

139

she could and should tell her husband and suddenly I had them, straight from Grandma's mouth although slightly edited to fit this situation.

'Here, in this country,' I said, 'we believe that a man's first loyalty must be to his wife ... as hers must be to her husband.' I said these words as authoritatively as if they were written into the Australian Constitution.

'Is that true?' Hanaka asked.

'Yes. A wife comes before anyone else, before the man's father or his *mother*. So you see it's alright to tell Alan.'

'I ... I will try ...' Hanaka said.

Today, Mother McDonald came with her friend, Olive. From the times of the ancient Greeks an olive branch has been a symbol of goodwill, but Mother McDonald's Olive came with a smile as false as her bitter black heart. Mother McDonald went to make tea, a task she had never before offered to do, and Olive, pretending to like me, said how surprised they all were when Alan announced his marriage to me because everyone knew he was about to become engaged to Carol O'Connor. Carol O'Connor was the most wonderful of girls, Olive proclaimed, and was still waiting for Alan.

With a chill running through my blood, I asked Olive why this Carol was waiting as Alan was now married to me. Olive patted my hand. 'These mixed marriages rarely work, my dear. When Alan realises he has a coloured baby rather than the blue-eyed blonde Carol could give him, I think you'll find yourself back in Japan.'

'Here's tea' Mother McDonald announced. 'You are pale, Hanaka, dear.'

'I'm afraid I might have said something to upset her,' Olive said.

'Dear me,' Mother McDonald replied, 'that is naughty of you, Olive.'

Louise says I must tell Alan. How can I do this? His mother will say it's not her fault that her friend said such terrible things. Louise says in Australia a man must choose his wife over his mother but the disharmony this would cause would be unbearable. Alan has always believed his mother would 'come around'. To 'come around' is the same as 'come to heel' but just as his brother's wife, Mary, did not 'come to heel' I know with a certainty as heavy as a closed iron gate that his mother will never 'come around'. What I do not know is whether I have the strength to fight this woman who so hates me. I wish to fall asleep and not wake until my baby is ready to be born and, when she is, I wish the world to be quite a different place.

33

A chilly kind of peace descended on our house. We all gave Maggie a very wide berth and she responded in kind, even taking her evening meal into her room and eating it there. Mum left it on the stove, the plate on top of a saucepan of water and covered by a saucepan lid to keep it warm. When speaking was absolutely necessary, we resorted to a stiff politeness as if we were very bad actors in a very bad film. Johnno and I worked on what we called our amazing invisible technique and most of the time it seemed to work – Maggie never indicated that she saw us and we pretended she wasn't there. So effective was this charade that Johnno nearly convinced himself that we really were invisible. Maggie and Dad did talk, but even that was strained. He was still upset with her but none of us wanted to fuel that fire because we were frightened he would get sick again. Mum said it was a good thing he had this job and could get out of the house and forget it all for a while. The first couple of weeks after Maggie went back to work had not gone well, if the violent slamming of doors as she re-entered the house was any indication, but she kept going every day and that's all any of us really cared about. Mum in particular was relieved because it was she who had to deal with the day-to-day reality of Maggie – feeding her, cleaning up after her, doing her washing and ironing. She could manage all that, but Maggie herself Mum had had enough of. One night I was surprised to see her coming out of

142

Maggie's room. She seemed flustered when she saw me. Later when we were in the kitchen together I asked her why she'd been in with Maggie.

'This is not good for any of us. I'm trying to get her to agree that one of us must live elsewhere.'

'If she buys us out, we'll have to move!'

'That wouldn't be the end of the world but I don't think she'll be able to get the money to do that.'

'What's the point then? We haven't got the money to buy her out.'

'There's a chance. Grandma and Uncle Tom have said they'll help.'

'Mum!'

'I didn't want to tell you until I knew exactly where it's all going but Lou, it's going to happen one way or another.'

'What does Maggie say?'

'Firstly, she claims the house is worth far more than it really is and of course wants us to pay this overinflated price and then she says she wants to buy us out and that maybe she can get a loan yet she never does anything about it.'

'It could go on forever!'

'It won't because I'm no longer prepared to live like this.'

'But if Maggie won't make up her mind or doesn't do anything, it could!'

'Then we'll ... we'll have to consider forcing the sale.'

'Can we do that?'

'Yes ... but it'll upset your father a great deal. I want to avoid that if possible.'

I was sure we were both thinking of his recent nightmare and how he'd almost slipped backwards, and maybe would have done so if his boss hadn't given him some time off.

'Mum? What happened to Dad ... who is Danny?'

'Danny was a boy who died in horrible circumstances. Your father ... that's when he won the medal, bringing the boy's body back.'

'What happened to him?'

143

'Louise. Believe me. There are things that happen in this world that are truly unspeakable.' I understood clearly that this subject was closed.

'If Maggie were to agree to us buying her out, your father would accept it, I think, but not if she's forced out.'

'She deserves to be forced out!'

'Try not to be so harsh in your judgments, Louise. Her help with your father was vital when he first came back from the war. I feel very sad for her in many ways ... she's lost so much.'

But my mother's words were lost on me. Not only did I judge Maggie harshly, I sought revenge for the havoc I believed she'd caused in our family and especially for the horrible words she'd said to Johnno who had always stuck up for her. As far as I was concerned I stood firmly on the high moral ground whereas Maggie had given up her right to be anything other than disrespected. As for my mother telling me or rather, not telling me the unspeakable which my father witnessed, I pondered what it could be, drawing upon all the horrors I knew of but as I began to frighten myself with these horrible images, I left it be.

I'd already discovered a few of Maggie's secrets as well as helping myself to her small change. She had a funny rubber thing with a nozzle which I knew was for douching because Libby had told me, and so now I knew that you could do something to stop getting pregnant. Before she'd told me, I didn't even know what douching meant and the whole thing still filled me with alarm and distaste. I also knew where Maggie kept her stash of money because Johnno told me that and although I'd never taken it out from its envelope, I knew it was a significant amount — between £200 and £300. I wondered why Maggie hadn't put that money in the bank and although I'd searched for her bank book I hadn't as yet found it. But I did find something else. Under a kind of ledge at the top of her wardrobe, Maggie had hidden two bottles of gin, one half empty. Mum had made no bones about there being no grog in the house, nor coming home after drinking, and not

144

since the 'dirty and drunk' incident had Maggie seemed affected by alcohol, but now I knew that although she'd not drunk so much for it to be obvious, neither could we assume that Maggie was sober. But I couldn't use this knowledge against Maggie unless I was prepared to acknowledge what I'd been doing.

I wanted to pay Maggie back. I wanted her gone from our lives. If Maggie was not altogether sober when she went to bed I figured her memory may not be as good as if she were.

I began a campaign to undermine her. It had to be done in a way that could never be traced back; it had to be done so that Maggie thought it was her memory or her own carelessness. One evening while Maggie was in the bath I stole one of her stockings. The next morning she fumed through the house asking Mum if she'd seen any stockings but Mum didn't wash Maggie's smalls. By the time she left for work, Maggie was running very late indeed. I'd hidden the stocking in my underpants and on the way to school I threw it over someone's back fence. I waited for more than a week and then I sneaked into her room after school and worked on a 'natural' loosening on one of the buttons of the two jackets she wore to work. This took longer than I'd thought and when I heard Mum pass the door my heart raced. Each time I went into Maggie's room, I took a sixpence, sometimes even more and checked the gin bottles, of which there were always two, with one in various degrees of emptiness. Wanting to know how much gin she was actually drinking overnight, I checked the bottles one afternoon and the next morning told Mum I had a stomach ache and felt as if I was going to be sick so she'd let me stay home. When Mum went to the shops I went into Maggie's room and found the proof – only one bottle remained – Maggie must have drunk half a bottle the night before and put the empty bottle in her handbag to dispose of in the same way I disposed of her stocking. Using a pin, I set to, carefully making a small run in a stocking that was draped over a chair.

Sometimes Oldie's words, '... watch out for ya aunt. She's a great hater ... ya need to keep out of her way' filtered

145

across my consciousness, but my resentment of Maggie was far stronger than the sense of danger I should have had.

34

School without Libby was as dull as a wet week, the word dull
being almost synonymous with slow. Even though Jenny and I
remained a close unit we both missed Libby's larking about as
well as her ability to attract boys to our triangle. Jenny was a
much quieter girl with an observant and irreverent sense of
humour and she worked harder at school than either of us,
getting excellent marks, whereas mine were simply good and
Libby's average. Frustrated at home with the lack of progress
about the house – Maggie had now decided to try for a loan,
so she said – and concerned for Hanaka whose mood was still
downcast, but mainly because I was bored without Libby, I
decided to work harder and better my marks.

Our new English teacher, Miss Marsden, fresh out of
university, auburn-haired, skin like a peach and a sparkling
diamond ring on her finger, had embarked on a crusade to
teach us young savages a thing or two about literature. She
set us the task of writing an essay on any book we really
loved.

'I want examples,' she said. 'Examples of where you
think the writing is particularly moving or real and why you like
it.' Miss Marsden's perfect bow-like lips painted in a soft coral
colour smiled at us, firmly convinced every kid in the class
would be raring to take up her challenge. It's true all of us
wanted to please her because most of us were in love with
her, but it was also true that most of us knew we would fail.

147

Not Jenny and me though – we decided we'd show Miss Marsden a thing or two. After all, she was the one who'd said, 'Don't hold back, Class.'

We were given a week to complete the essay and so intent was I to impress, I decided not to visit Hanaka until I'd finished. When I called in to tell her this she was almost desperately pleased to see me which made me alarmed that something else bad had happened, but Hanaka said no.

'I have ... not been able to ...' Here Hanaka stopped.

'To what?' I asked.

'To concentrate. Yes, concentrate ... Instead I can think only of ...'

Of Mother McDonald's nastiness? Of her homeland? Her baby and the half and half business? Hanaka sat down and said no more.

'Has the old witch visited?' I asked.

Hanaka gave me a ghost of a smile and shook her head.

'Alan told her that I must rest quietly and have no visitors.'

'You told Alan?'

'A little ...'

'That's good ...'

'But soon I will have to see her again and, when the baby comes, I do not want her to be near my baby.'

Oh my goodness me! Hanaka was in a terrible state. Might she be having a ... a nervous collapse? If my father got sick in the mind because of the war and unspeakable things, couldn't Hanaka get sick in the same way? She may have experienced things that were unspeakable too, even if those horrors were slightly different. But ... but shouldn't she feel safe here? With her husband in her new country? No, not necessarily, because Dad was safe too, but that hadn't stopped his sickness. Sometimes, even though he was much better now, certain events could, yes, lately for Dad it had been Maggie's behaviour ... so couldn't Mother McDonald's behaviour be the 'certain events' that were, as Grandma liked

148

to say, 'the straw that broke the camel's back'? This was all way more serious than I felt cut out for. What on earth was I going to do? All these thoughts crashed around in my head as I watched my hopeful, brave, dignified and beautiful friend give in to despair.

What I did surprised even me. I went to see Mrs Parker, the Quaker lady. I had to tell someone! Some adult who might know what to do or who might speak to Alan.

'Ah,' she said when she saw me standing on her doorstep. 'The mystery girl.' Although unnerved by Mrs Parker's greeting and her sharp look, I went inside and blurted out that I was worried about Hanaka. 'She's too sad,' I said.

'Why do you think this is so?' Mrs Parker asked. Although still sharp, I knew then that she had noticed the change in Hanaka too and was concerned.

'It's her mother-in-law ... she's unkind!' Mrs Parker sighed as if my words simply reinforced something she already knew.

'Dear, this is a very delicate matter ... really not our business ... family and all that ...' Was she going to do *nothing*? Where was her godliness? If she said she'd pray for Hanaka, I'd ... I'd ...

'You and I must make a plan of action, dear. We must help our little friend ...' I could have hugged her and even when she said, as I was leaving, 'We must seek Guidance,' I didn't feel at all like kicking her in the shins. From then on, I called her Divine D, though not to her face.

So it was that I spent every afternoon for the next week in Hanaka's house, me writing my English essay and Hanaka continuing her painting. Sometimes she rested on the couch and then I would read to her from what I'd written and ask her if it made sense or if I should change this word or that, anything at all to keep her from falling into what seemed a mournful reverie. I was only one part of the plan Divine D executed – the Friends had been called in as well as the friends of the Friends and Hanaka had visitors every day, visitors who sat calmly knitting or reading while she painted.

149

Sometimes the artist who taught her took her and a few of his other students to the Dandenongs or to Heidelberg to paint for the whole day. Divine D's plan was for Hanaka to be kept busy and to make sure she was *never* alone with her witchy mother-in-law. When Alan told Hanaka he might have to go to Adelaide for his work, we made sure that Hanaka's plans to stay with Naoko were made well in advance. All this was very well, as Divine D said, but we couldn't do it forever. Divine D was determined to speak to Alan about his wife's fragile health as soon as the right opportunity presented itself.

I wrote my essay on *For Whom the Bell Tolls* and Jenny did *Far from the Madding Crowd*. Neither of us held back, well, I did a little, not making too much of the earth moving parts, and Miss Marsden was so pleased that we ended up in her Form 5 English class once a week. This proved a mixed blessing. The 'blessing' part was that we got to be with the older boys who previously we'd only been able to look at wistfully from afar; the 'mixed' part was that our essays were read by the entire class as an example of impassioned writing! While both of us were beyond mortification, we were also very pleased with ourselves which made us braver than we'd normally be with these almost-grown-up kids. Both Jenny and I immediately fell in love, fortunately with different boys, and our new-found braveness helped us not to be stupidly tongue-tied with these boys. My boy's name was Jonathan and he was small and dark as well as being very clever and seventeen! He came from England. The problem was that although he plainly liked me it was rather as an older brother might. Jenny said this was because I was too young and because of that he couldn't like me in a romantic way which didn't mean he didn't. Jonathan was the first boy I'd really liked since Toluk and I wanted him to like me in a non-brotherly way. Mum had tried to get me to go to her church youth club but I said no because I knew the boys there would be wet socks. Jenny was luckier with her boy as she was fifteen already and her boy, sixteen, but as he hadn't shown any of the signs necessary to prove that he liked her too, she was also unlucky.

With all this going on, home became a much less difficult place for me, and although the strain between my mother and Maggie was still apparent, Maggie and Dad were once more on good terms. Although Johnno was a little more reserved with Maggie than before, he too seemed to have forgiven her, but I thought that was because Maggie had cajoled them both by reminiscing about her and Dad's childhood – *Remember, Jack, when Mum and I held you down to take off the socks you'd worn, we reckoned, for a good month?* Johnno loved to hear stories about Dad when he was a boy. Maggie had come back to the dinner table and even sometimes sang along with Dad and Johnno but if that happened both Mum and I made up some excuse to leave the room. I concentrated on my schoolwork which was beginning to bring me good marks and I found I liked being thought of as clever. I liked it too that my cleverness impressed Jonathan as well as amused him. He called me a precocious brat, which was almost the same as saying he liked me a lot, but I wanted more from him than that!

35

The problem of Hanaka remained unsolved and worrying. While she was quite a lot brighter, all her friends were getting somewhat exhausted in their attempts to keep her out of Mother McDonald's clutches. Divine D tried to encourage her to tell Alan how she felt about Mother McDonald and why, but Hanaka, whilst saying she'd told Alan, left me in no doubt that she'd told him very little. Divine D was getting impatient with the situation in a most un-divine way.

'Is the man blind as well as stupid?' she asked.

I laughed, but it was the question I'd asked myself. Surely Alan could see that Hanaka was very unhappy. Divine D still hadn't spoken to Alan, and when I pressed her as to when she would all she'd said was, 'Ah, dear ... It's not as simple as that ...'

'Once Alan knows, he'll do something ... he'll protect her ...'

'That's what we want him to do, but are we positive he will? What if he takes his mother's side? What if he doesn't believe his wife?'

'Then he's a bad person,' I said.

'No, no ... He may find it impossible to go against his mother ... which would be a very bad result for us but it wouldn't necessarily make him a bad person.'

I definitely disagreed with her.

'Also, people don't take kindly to other people telling them what's wrong in their family. We don't want to lose her, do we?'

We decided that I'd have one more try to persuade Hanaka to tell Alan the truth before Divine D gave him 'a good talking to'.

How kind people have been ... I try to repay this kindness by doing as they wish, being as agreeable as I can, painting too, even though my heart is not in it ... yet all the time ... I cannot rid myself of a feeling of impending disaster ... How this disaster will come I do not know but what I fear, dread, is that it will come through my mother-in-law and it will harm my baby. Then I think I am losing my senses, that I have imagined the words Olive spoke, perhaps even imagined that Olive was doing Mother McDonald's bidding. I am under the water and trying, trying to get to the surface. She rings at night and speaks to Alan. 'Mum's upset that you're never home. Can't you make some time for her?' He is puzzled ... he does not wish to be displeased with me but he cannot understand. 'I know Mum sometimes says hurtful things ... but she doesn't mean them, Hanaka ... She's trying ... Can't you try too?' I am trying ... so hard everything strains ... my heart ... bursting ... I push my way to the surface and then ... I am again down at the bottom my breath almost gone ... my lungs filling ... I will drown ... my lungs burning ... I am drowning ... my baby ... I must ... must push up ... up ... to the light ... try ... to the light ... my baby ...

Distracted thinking about how I'd get Hanaka to confide in me and worried that Divine D might put her foot in it with Alan and cause us all to be outcast, I almost didn't register that Oldie

153

was in our garden. So intent was he on reading a magazine that he didn't see me either.

'I'm goin' to get one of these beauties,' Oldie said. He often had a chat with himself.

'What beauties?' I asked, thinking to startle him.

'These, Girlie ... look here ...' Had he seen me after all? He pointed to an advertisement in the magazine. I read, 'Something new and rare in native plants. "The Maffra Bottlebrush." '

'Do you like native plants?' I asked, surprised.

'Love 'em. My own garden's almost all natives ...'

'But I thought you liked our garden ... and what about Japanese plants? You seemed really interested in them ... '

'All plants are interestin'... but you know Girlie, this isn't Blighty or Japan. I like plants to belong in their geography ... ya know what I mean? And natives bring the native birds too – lorikeets, wattlebirds, magpies ... '

I sort of knew what Oldie meant but ... 'You think natives are more beautiful?'

'Some are ...'

'More beautiful than ... than a ... a Therese Bugnet rose ...?'

'Blimey, Girlie ...'

' "Beautiful deep pink that gets softer – unusual crossing of Old World roses ... " '

'Who told ya that?

'Mrs Parker ... I call her Divine D ... '

'Sounds good. But what about the wattle when it's out? A sight for sore eyes!'

'A ... a poplar ...?'

'Beautiful but so is a snow gum ...'

'A maple ...?'

'Glorious ... yes ... especially in autumn ...You've got me there, Girlie ... but it might be because of that reading I told you about ... got me kind of fascinated and I've found out more ... about when Jap plants first came here ...' Oldie went back to his magazine.

154

'When?'

'What?'

'When did they come here?'

'Well, apparently, after the Yanks made the Japs open their country to trading, a nursery in Yokohama, which is a port city near Tokyo, started to send plants to Australia ... about 1890 if I remember rightly. There was a huge interest from nurserymen here to have these plants and in Sydney there was even a nursery which specialised in Bonsai – ya know what that is, Girlie?'

'Little trees?'

'Big trees made to be little by pruning the branches and roots. It's a real skilled thing ... originally from China ... Don't like it much ... too unnatural for me.' He turned again to the magazine.

'I'm going to get one of these ...' Oldie was back with the Maffra Bottlebrush.

Later that day Mum said Oldie had forgotten his magazine and she'd put it on the hall-stand to give him when next he came. In passing, I noticed it was called *The Australian Garden Lover*, but I didn't stop to look at it. I was too concerned about my upcoming mission to persuade Hanaka to tell her husband the truth about his mother, rather than it coming to him from Divine, who he may think is nothing but a nasty nosy Parker.

As well as all this, I'd rashly agreed to go to Jonathan's house, knowing full well that neither his mother nor father would be home. Thinking of my rather subtle, I liked to think, flirting, and of my initial pledge to seduce him, I was almost too afraid to imagine what might happen when we were alone. Even though I'd told myself Jonathan didn't show his true feelings for me because of our age difference, he'd never been more than a very friendly friend so perhaps both my fears and my hopes were a fantasy. I certainly didn't want to risk humiliating myself by being too bold with him and being rebuffed. I wanted very badly to go to his house and I wanted not to go, but not quite as badly.

155

To cover my visit to Jonathan's I'd told Mum that Jenny and I were meeting Libby. Jenny was, and I felt a bit bad that I wasn't, but Jen said Libby would understand. She'd made me promise to tell her everything that happened. I was on my way out the door when I heard Maggie call from the lounge room. 'You're all dolled up – where're you going?' she asked in a normal voice. I very much wanted to ignore her question but knew that might cause more problems than answering her.

'Out with Jenny from school.'

'Bull!'

I was determined to ignore her but Maggie was not one to be ignored if she chose so.

'I'm going to catch you one day ... you see if I don't!' How much of that gin had she drunk?

'There's nothing to catch,' I replied.

'Think you're smart, eh?' My aunt's voice now held menace. I noticed then that her tea mug and ashtray were sitting on Oldie's magazine.

'That's Oldie's,' I said, attempting to move it but Maggie put out her hand to prevent me.

'Stupid old coot,' she retorted.

Quick, hot anger flashed through me. 'Give it to me! It's not yours!'

'Oops,' she said as she deliberately spilled her tea over the magazine. 'All you had to do was ask politely.'

I snatched the magazine from her and stalked out the door, Maggie's coarse laughter behind me.

Perhaps this encounter contributed to what happened at Jonathan's house. Perhaps not. It transpired that Jonathan was a far more sophisticated boy than the boy he showed at school. Jonathan told me that when he got to University he was going to make love to as many women as he could. He told me I was really smart and beautiful but our age difference made it impossible. Then everything happened very quickly.

'I bet you don't even know what making love is,' he said.

I protested that I did but Jonathan only laughed at me.

156

It was Jonathan's laughter and his lightness that made me unafraid – not like I felt when Toluk and I were down by the creek. 'I'll show you,' Jonathan said taking out a book that had a pen drawing on the front. He turned each page slowly pointing out what I could eye-poppingly see. Drawings of horrible little men with huge penises! Men and women having sex such as I'd never been able to imagine it even after my encounter with Toluk, but certainly showing me *exactly* what happened. All the time Jonathan stroked my arm working his way to my breast, neck, then downwards to my thighs. I was hot and breathless and ...

'You're excited, aren't you,' Jonathon crooned, placing my hand on his penis. I almost recoiled but then his hands were between my legs.

'Don't worry, Brat. Nothing's going to go too far but I'll show you how to feel nice,' he said, and he did. I left Jonathan's house that afternoon worldlier than when I'd entered it.

Jonathan warned me that the book he'd shown me was banned in Australia and that I must never tell anyone, so Jenny missed out. She missed out too on the details of my instructive experience of sexual pleasure. I told her that Jonathan and I had kissed a lot but he'd said he was too old for me.

'It must have been a lot because you look like the cat that's got the cream,' Jenny commented.

36

Our 'borrowed landscape', the apple tree, was discarding its blossoms for unspoiled new leaves and stood old and proud, ready to lend itself to the Japanese garden. Luckily trees don't have eyes because the only change from the time Oldie had dug up the garden was the addition of two spindly looking azaleas. If I were the apple tree, I'd surely lend my beauty elsewhere! If I couldn't help Hanaka resolve the Mother McDonald problem the garden might stay this way forever.

'Hanaka is more likely to tell you how she feels than anyone else. She trusts you,' Divine D said as I'd nervously received instructions before the big talk. '*That woman* was there the other day. I was looking out for her arrival and went in after about ten minutes. I can tell you *that woman* didn't like it one bit but I stayed for as long as I could. At least I gave her less time to torment poor Hanaka.'

Poor Divine D! How she must long to call Mother McDonald what she was – a nasty, cruel, bloody old bitch!

I started off the conversation with Hanaka by praising the old apple tree and commenting favourably on the azaleas. Then I needed to get to the point.

'Mrs Parker – Dorothy – said you had a visitor yesterday – one who's not welcome?'

'You must not say that, Louise. She is my mother-in-law. It is for me to find a way to please her.'

Bull! As Maggie would say! 'You've been a wonderful daughter-in-law! What does she want?'

'For me to be ...'

'To be? What?'

'I am not who she wants ...'

'You're who Alan wants ...'

'Soon, maybe he too ...'

'Is he cross with you?'

'No ... no ... but he cannot understand ...'

'If he doesn't understand, you must make him! *Tell* him what it's really like ...'

'It would cause so much trouble ... She ... she wants me to go ....' Hanaka's voice was really low and I didn't catch the last word.

'Go where?'

Hanaka said nothing.

'Hanaka, where does she want you to go?'

'Away.' It was a whisper.

'She said that?' Hanaka nodded. *That woman* was a *wicked* bloody old bitch!

'She wants Alan to marry Carol O'Connor ...'

Who, for Pete's sake was this Carol O'Connor?

'She said they were engaged before the war and this Carol is still waiting for ...'

'Alan's *your* husband ...!'

Piece by piece the story came out, my outrage growing at every revelation, particularly that *that woman* had used someone else to do her dirty work. I was almost made mute by the sheer malice of it. Although I urged Hanaka to reveal what she told me to her husband, for the first time it came to me that this wasn't a simple matter of Hanaka telling her husband the truth about his mother. Mother McDonald wasn't going to give in! Despite my new worldliness this was definitely uncharted territory for me and I needed more advice from Divine D.

Divine D was aghast at what I told her.

'I'm at a loss,' she said to my dismay. '*That woman* seems to be set on ... on destroying our girl!'

159

Over a cuppa and freshly made tea-cake with a delicious sugar and cinnamon topping, Divine D ruminated on what could be done. It was, she said, an even more complicated situation than we'd suspected and she would have to think very carefully about what to do. She agreed that Mother McDonald wasn't going to give in which meant that for Alan to take Hanaka's word, he must label his mother a liar. But what if he didn't take his wife's word? 'That would be disaster for Hanaka,' Divine D said. 'That beastly woman will use Hanaka's mental problems against her.'

'Mental problems...?' I asked. Although I'd feared that possibility myself, when Dorothy spoke the words it became more of a terrible reality. The cake suddenly lost its appeal.

'Dear, for someone to be in such a state of ... of ... defeat ... I think there's a mental problem ... Maybe she's been through too much ... Her father's suicide ... leaving her alone except for the rather rigid aunt, the war ... hunger ... terrible strain ... and then trying to fit in here.'

Dorothy sighed. 'What worries me is that if they start calling Hanaka 'mad' – well known in the past for women who cause problems – she's not a citizen yet – it's possible she could be deported ...'

'Her baby ...?'

Dorothy stood up suddenly, cake crumbs falling onto the carpet.

'Her baby will be a citizen but what if ...? I wouldn't put anything past *that* woman!'

'Hanaka isn't causing problems!' I protested.

'Ah, yes she is, my dear. To *that* woman Hanaka *is* the problem! What to do? What to do?'

Poor Divine. Surely it was bad for a woman of her age to get so agitated? She'd make herself sick. Then I had a brainwave. Why hadn't I thought of it before? 'Naoko,' I said. Naoko had recently moved to Brisbane which I'd been glad about but now I longed for her to be back here. 'Couldn't we ask her to come and stay with Hanaka?'

160

❖

I long to sleep ... a long dark sleep ... not a sleep that assails me with bad dreams that I awake from with a pounding heart ... then fearful of the shadows ... of what lurks within these shadows ... no, no, they are only harmless tricks of light and dark ... harmless tricks ... menacing shadows ... destructive spirits I can no longer hide from ... I long for safety but when I close my eyes my dreams are filled with monsters ... my baby ... my baby ... I must fight but I am so tired ... too tired ... I long for sleep ... sleep that never wakes to shadows ... the deepest black silk of ... oblivion ...

37

Bruised by my latest encounter with Maggie and feeling helpless and frustrated at what was happening to Hanaka, I embarked on another round of mischief in Maggie's room. There I found rich pickings. Since my last visit Maggie had gotten even more careless with her loose change and I easily picked up 2 shillings in small amounts that would not be missed. When I checked the gin cache I also searched the other side of the top of the wardrobe and there I found another of Maggie's secrets – a packet of Relaxa-Tabs. I knew from advertisements that these tablets were for 'worry, overwork, grief and sleeplessness'. My resentment, indeed, even hatred of Maggie allowed me no compassion; I couldn't see her as a sick woman who was suffering grief even if its manifestation was unpalatable to those around her. Instead Maggie was irrevocably linked in my mind with Hanaka's persecution, as I believed with reasonable certainty that Hanaka would be treated just as badly or even worse than she was by her mother-in-law, by my own aunt. I wanted to punish Maggie as I wanted to punish Mother McDonald, even Alan for his inability to see what was staring him in the face: the inevitable collapse of Hanaka and the life she'd hoped for, the life I believed she deserved.

During the next week I regularly went into Maggie's room and stole small amounts of her change. There was always more money scattered about than I'd remembered being there previously which I put down to Maggie's drinking and pill taking. I was hoping against hope that she'd slip up soon, initiating a crisis which would give the stalled plans for selling the house a big boost. That was another major frustration – Maggie had wriggled her way back into Dad's good books and although selling the house was ostensibly still on the agenda, in reality she had made no real moves to either buy the house or sell it to my father. This was becoming an agony for my mother who'd seen the possibility of a home without Maggie becoming a reality, and whose every instinct strained toward that end.

At school Jonathan acted even more like a big brother but now his conversation included meaning for me alone. 'Hello, Brat,' he'd said when we'd met for the first time at school after that afternoon at his house. 'Read any good books lately?' As for what had happened between us, I alternated between urgently wanting it to happen again and planning how to avoid it.

When a week went by without me having to make an excuse to avoid Jonathan's entreaty to come to his house again, because he hadn't asked me to, I was completely confused, not having a clue what I really wanted to do. Jenny had said I'd looked like a cat that got the cream and, although I sensed that too much cream could be a bad thing, what about a cat that didn't get any cream at all?

I told Jenny that Jonathan hadn't made any suggestions that we meet again. 'Maybe it's because he knows that if he doesn't ask you, you'll want to more,' she said. 'So when eventually he does, you'll be desperate to go. My mum reckons it's a very old trick men play on girls.'

I then asked the question that all girls dread to ask their girlfriends.

'Do you like him, Jen?'

'I don't *not* like him but ... he's ... well, he's lived in Europe ... his mother's a musician and she's supposed to be, you know, very ... unusual.'

'But that makes him interesting ...'

163

'Yes, but he's *seventeen* and he *knows* so much more than we do *and* it would have to be secret ... I mean, you've proved he likes you ... Maybe if you were sixteen ... '

Although my head, even my heart, accepted that Jenny was right, whenever Jonathan looked my way my body took on a life of its own remembering those hours on his bed.

It was in such a mixed-up state that I saw the mouse on the path at the side of our house. It was very dead, so dead it had become desiccated, its mouse-like being reduced to a fragile lightness. I didn't wonder how it came to be there and because of my own squeamishness certainly wouldn't have used it as I did if it had been in a lesser but more putrid state of decay. Carefully I placed the mouse onto a piece of paper and, after checking where everyone was in the house, I went into Maggie's room and gently deposited it on the top of the packet of Relaxa-Tabs. I tried to estimate when Maggie would find it but I didn't know whether she took the tablets at night or in the morning. I really hoped I'd hear her scream.

I was not disappointed. As I was coming out to the kitchen for breakfast I heard a shriek and a moment later Maggie stormed into the kitchen with the reason for the shriek in a piece of newspaper. 'How did it get there?' she shouted. I shrugged. Mum asked her what she meant and Johnno's face registered a number of emotions before his eyes settled with alarm on me.

Fortunately Mum somewhat soothed Maggie by saying the mouse must have been there for a very long time to be so dried-out but Maggie still wanted to know how it got there.

'Where, Maggie? Show us where the mouse was.' I looked as innocent as I could but when Maggie hastily said it didn't matter, it must have fallen down from the wardrobe into an open drawer, I couldn't suppress a small smirk of triumph. Johnno came into my room wearing his scrunched-up look.

'You shouldn't have done that, Lou,' he scolded.

'Done what?'

'It was my mouse ... and then I dropped it and didn't know where ...'

164

'It must have been another mouse, Johnno,' I said. I could tell he wanted to believe that. 'I wouldn't do that ...'

'Promise, Lou, you won't do anything anymore,' Johnno said. 'It'll only make Maggie angrier.'

38

Naoko was coming! Divine D and I were elated by the news and if Hanaka could have seen us dancing around Divine D's lounge room she would have thought we had both gone quite mad, but it was relief that made us dance. We were also relieved that Hanaka seemed so much calmer and was pleased Naoko was coming to stay for several weeks. Hanaka also told me that she'd spoken to Alan. When I asked what he was going to do, Hanaka said he had a plan and, she said, 'Everything will be alright soon.' Privately I thought the problems were a lot more complicated but as Hanaka was relaxed, almost happy, I dared not say anything to upset that. Divine D agreed with me but she was also surprised that the problems Hanaka faced, as we understood them, were to be, apparently, so very easily solved.

As Naoko was not able to come for two more weeks I spent as much time as I could with Hanaka. With her newfound calmness had come a rather dream-like state as if she were somewhere far away and it slightly troubled me. When I asked her about the Japanese garden she seemed for a moment not to know what I was talking about. Telling myself it was because of her pregnancy I decided that to get Hanaka's attention back into the present I would need to come up with something special for the garden.

That night I read Oldie's tea-stained gardening magazine which I'd been minding until next time he came. I

166

passed the Maffra Bottlebrush and then read *Silver Birch. Large trees 12ft – 70/- Claret Ash. Large 15/- 20/- + 30/-* but these trees weren't what I was looking for. Finally I found it:

Maples
Acer Purpurea (Purple foliage)
Acer Versicolour (green and pink)
Acer Palmatum (Scarlet autumn foliage)
15/- to 25/-   Mature trees – £5 – £6

A sudden irrepressible desire flooded me to have the now bereft Japanese garden made whole, no longer a figment of fancy or of need, but a resplendent place created by Hanaka and me. For this to have any chance of happening we first needed a splendid mature maple tree to be the centrepiece. And we needed it now.

So began another round of deception, fairly careful deception except in the case of stealing from Maggie. That I carelessly executed by taking £5 in the course of little more than a week. Adding that to the £2 I'd already stolen from her, I began the necessary lies to enable my longing to become reality.

Oldie agreed to buy the tree on behalf of my friend whose garden he'd dug and who'd had the misfortune of a broken-legged husband. He said he'd bring soil too, to make the small hill where the tree was to be planted. I pointed out the advertisement in his ratty-looking magazine.

'I reckon I can get it cheaper at another nursery. The tree – they want me to plant it?'

'Yes, but make the hill first, then put the tree on the side a bit.'

'You're the gardener now, are you, Girlie? I know what to do first. Important to plant a tree right,' Oldie said.

'How long will it take?'

'Dunno... an hour or two ... '

What was I going to do with Hanaka while Oldie planted the tree?

'How's that leg goin'?'

I wasn't to be caught on the hop this time. 'Better now.'

I had it! Divine D could take Hanaka shopping.

Oldie said he'd get the tree and soil during the next week and would then like to plant it as soon as possible. I still had to work out what to tell Hanaka about where the tree came from as I couldn't say that I'd bought it for her. Also I needed Oldie to follow instructions – mine – so I told him he should tell me before he went to my friend's house.

'She's having a baby and some days aren't ... good for her ...' I lamely explained. Oldie looked at me with his shrewd dark eyes.

'Whatever you say, Girlie.'

So it was that a few days later when I went around to the back door of Hanaka's house I almost fell down in shock. Hanaka was delighted at both my shock and my reason for it. *There, in front of the borrowed landscape of the old apple tree was the most perfect hill on which, planted slightly to one side, stood a perfectly shaped maple.*

'Your friend Mr Oldie gave it to us! Is it not the most lovely of trees?'

I was still speechless but Hanaka was so much like her old self that the anger I'd felt rising gave way to delight which only lasted a minute before anxiety took its place.

'You spoke to him?'

'Mr Oldie said he was given the tree as payment for a job and as he had no room for it in his own garden he thought we might like it ... I tried to give him some money but he would not take anything ... He is a very kind gentleman ...   I will leave him a gift.' Hanaka laughed then, such as I hadn't heard for some time, but higher, excited.

I was stunned. Now that Oldie knew about Hanaka he must also know that the £7 did not belong to her. Whose money did he think it was? Could he suspect? He must! I was in the deepest of trouble!

'Mr Oldie said you were a very good girl with a naughty streak,' Hanaka laughed. 'I think that is true! Do not look so worried. Mr Oldie likes you very much ... I could tell ... and your whole family.'

168

Oldie must have been pretending to Hanaka when he said that because surely now I was the only member of my family he didn't like. What was I going to do? I'd tell Oldie ... I'd ... I'd say ... All at once I didn't have the heart to go on with it. Lying to good people, people I cared about, the lies becoming more and more extreme and the scheming only ending up muddled and stupid. What was I doing?

'You are so pale Louise. Sit, sit here because I have another surprise for you. Then I will make tea.'

I wanted to sit on Hanaka's couch forever, or at least for as long as I could, because when I got home I'd be exposed, shamed ... I didn't know how I'd bear it ... I began to plan on going to Jenny's house and spinning yet another story and staying the night but Mum and Dad and poor Johnno ... they'd be so desperate ... Then Hanaka was before me, more beautiful than I'd ever seen her, a perfect Japanese bride in her mother's wedding *kimono*.

'Hanaka ...' I almost didn't have words. 'You're ... you're ...'

'You have wanted to see me wear this *kimono* for a very long time, Louise ...'

'It ... and you are so beautiful ... Thank you ...'

'I thank you my dear little sister for being such a friend to me.' She bowed before me and I stood and returned the bow.

'Soon everything will be alright,' I said, believing that to be true for Hanaka if not for myself. I would never be allowed out of the house again. By the time I could escape at eighteen Hanaka's baby would already be four years old! To stop these thoughts I concentrated only on Hanaka, a vision in white silk before me, on the detail in the small embroidered flowers and the scarlet silk lining which showed when Hanaka moved, the same colour of blood pumped from the heart. I longed to stay in this moment forever.

'Would you like, Louise? You may if you would like.'

I took off my shoes and jumper ready for when Hanaka came back from her bedroom with the wedding *kimono* for me to try on.

In the short time it took for disaster to befall, I can recall almost everything that happened but the chilling moment when I first heard her voice remains a permanent stain in my mind.

'Get out here, you bloody little thief,' Maggie bellowed, banging on the door. I could not move. Hanaka came out of the bedroom still in the *kimono* and looked at me in confusion and fear. I gestured for her to be quiet hoping that Maggie might give up and go away.

'If you're not out here in one minute you little bitch, I'm calling the police! You'll end up in a home! I mean it! Come out now or I'll call the cops!'

I could tell from Maggie's voice that she was drunk but, more importantly, that she was extremely dangerous and I must do as she said or she would call the police.

'Get out here! I know all about it ... the money, the mouse, the tree ...' Oldie had betrayed me?

'Made your bloody spying little brother tell me. I said I'd make sure you went to jail unless ...' Vomit filled my mouth.

Hanaka tried to stop me opening the front door.

'No, Louise! I will call the police.'

'Sorry, so sorry ... Stay inside ... please Hanaka ...' But as I went outside to face my deranged aunt, Hanaka came behind me.

'Well, well, well, what have we got here? Tokyo Rose!' Maggie grabbed my arm in a vice-like grip which I struggled to free myself from but could not, while Hanaka made small forays toward Maggie, trying to get her to give me up. As Maggie struck back at Hanaka, I was truly terrified.

'Go back inside, Hanaka! Please!'

'Maybe I'd better call the police after all,' Maggie said. 'Maybe Tokyo Rose here is involved too.' I hit Maggie then, with my free hand, hit her square in her face with a force I never knew I possessed. 'You fuckin' little bitch!' Maggie

170

grabbed me and twisted my arm up behind my back making me yelp in pain. Blood trickled from her nose.

'In the car!' she shouted and marched me over to it. 'One move and it'll be to the cop shop.' I knew she meant it.

Hanaka was standing in her front garden, strangely still and staring straight ahead. Suddenly, urgently, something she'd said came into my mind. 'I need to help her,' I pleaded with Maggie. 'She's pregnant and she's, she's ...' Maggie's laugh was poison. I have never hated anyone as much as I hated my aunt at that moment. I tried to break away but she pushed me to the ground and pulled my arm so hard I felt sick with pain. When I next looked, Hanaka was no longer there. A truck was coming down the street, not just any truck but one named Pamela. Oldie jumped out of the truck and ran toward me and Maggie. I screamed at Oldie, 'It's Hanaka! Go to her now! I think she's going to ...' and Oldie, understanding the absolute desperation in my voice even if not exactly why, was off. As Maggie drove me away I caught a glimpse of Divine D hurrying along the footpath toward Hanaka's.

Sobbing hysterically, my arm throbbing, we reached home. Before we'd even got to the front gate, Maggie grabbed me again in a muscle-man grip and began shouting for my mother. Mum flew through the front door, pulling me away from Maggie, aghast at the sight of her badly dishevelled relations, one weeping, the other bleeding and drunk.

'Bloody dirty lyin' thief, ya daughter,' Maggie informed my mother, slurring her words.

'Quickly! Get inside!' Mum ordered us.

'The Jap bitch's in it too! You can thank *your* lucky stars I didn't get the cops.'

My mother, who I'd often wished was more ... more ... and less ... less ... was in no mood to be thanking her lucky stars.

'I will not have my family endure you for one more minute, Maggie! I want you out of this house in an hour!'

'It's her fault!' Maggie pointed at me. 'She's a real little lyin' ...'

171

'I don't care what she's done, Maggie. This is not how to deal with it.'

'Who do ya fuckin' think ya are? This is my house and ya not gettin' me out! You've always thought you were better than me ...'

'The house is being sold with or without your consent. I'm ringing the doctor now and if you don't want him to see you here after what you've done to my daughter or for me to charge *you* with assaulting her, you'd better get going!'

'Jack'll never ...'

'Jack will do what I say!'

Later, soothed by the sedative Dr Martin gave me and by my mother's gentle washing of my face, arms, and dirty, bloodied knees, I became sleepy. Johnno sitting at the end of my bed, his little face a portrait of shock, was the last thing I saw before oblivion claimed me. But on waking early next day, the blissful non-state before full consciousness came was brutally torn away by the awful realisation that Hanaka had wanted to and attempted to take her own life. Last night Mum had told me, 'The Japanese woman will be alright.' Lying there, I knew that *couldn't* be true. How could Hanaka *ever* be alright again?

Part Two

1

In the weeks following what I called 'the catastrophe' and my family called 'this mess' I lay in bed wishing, if not exactly for death, at least amnesia. I knew Hanaka was in hospital and recovering because Mum told me so every day. I didn't ask for details because I couldn't bear facing up to the reality of what had happened and the part I'd played. My mother never offered other details either.

It was the threat by Dr Martin that he'd send me to hospital to be fed by intravenous drip that got me eating again. Mum cooked me fluffy cheese omelettes and scrambled eggs, tender pieces of meat with creamy mashed potato as well as custards and jellied fruit – much the same foods she'd made for me when I'd had two back teeth out. My official diagnosis now was 'nervous exhaustion'.

In those first couple of weeks Johnno constantly popped in and out of my room to give me titbits of the happenings in our household. He wasn't supposed to disturb me as Dr Martin had ordered bed rest and a ban on any talk of the events that led me to my bed. But Johnno couldn't help himself, he was full of the drama as well as upset by Maggie's leaving and, whenever I bothered to open my eyes and look, his little face was all pinched up.

'Oldie and that lady came to see Mum this morning. They talked about you and the Japanese lady ... but when

Mum saw me listening she made me go away,' he told me one day.

I also learned that Maggie was on a 'holiday'. Knowing that Maggie wasn't in the house filled me with both relief and a sense of victory, a victory which the very second I felt the pleasure of it, turned to guilt. Sometimes I grunted acknowledgment of Johnno's news but often I didn't answer at all. It was as if these goings-on were happening on the other side of impenetrable glass. One day Johnno announced. 'Grandma's coming tomorrow and Uncle Tom next week.' That news made the glass seem not so thick after all and I burrowed further down in the blankets. Even though I longed for Grandma's determined clarity, I feared her disapproval more.

It was only at night that I let myself cry for Hanaka and myself – knowing that we would never again be as we were. She now knew of my myriad lies and deceptions, probably knew me too to be a thief – I'd learned from her that to steal was considered a great failing by the Japanese. That *she* knew I was a liar and a thief was far *far* worse than my mother or even Grandma Henderson knowing – they *had* to love me, but Hanaka wasn't obliged to. Worst of all, I believed that if I hadn't stolen from Maggie to buy the maple tree, Hanaka may not have attempted suicide. Like an underground spring my tears seeped out soaking the pillow, but when they finally stopped, I slept deep and dark.

One night, very late, I heard Johnno come into my room. I pretended to be asleep. He crept close to my bed and whispered, 'I love you, Lou. Please get better soon,' before running back down the hall. Some nights later when Johnno came in repeating his mantra, I held the bedclothes up and quick as a flash he snuggled down with me, two hurt animals finding comfort in each other's warmth. No one else knew of this arrangement until Johnno, the family early bird, slept in one morning. Mum told me later that everyone breathed a huge sigh of relief because they knew then I'd be alright.

176

One morning I awoke and *had* to know. I shouted for Mum so loudly that she came rushing.

'Tell me, Mum!' My voice sounded odd, harsh but fragile too. After being ordered to calm down or Dr Martin would put me into hospital, Mum told what she knew.

It turned out that our quiet leafy suburb did run to heroines – and heroes – after all. We could proudly boast our very own versions of Mr Darcy and Colonel Brandon, of Melanie Wilkes and Scarlett O'Hara. That our heroic people were neither beautiful nor young didn't matter at all.

'The Japanese woman,' Mum said, 'wouldn't open the door, so Oldie broke a window and got into the house that way. He could smell gas, so he turned that off first, and then found the bathroom door was locked – Oldie has a sore shoulder now – but fortunately the lock wasn't very strong. Mrs Parker knows first-aid, so she was able to stop the ...' That's when I understood that Hanaka had slit her wrists. It made me feel sick.

'It's my entire fault,' I cried.

'No! It was nothing to do with you, or Maggie! She'd planned it for weeks!'
Apparently Hanaka had left two letters, both dated three weeks before my aunt's rampage.

'I must see her!'

But Dr Martin had given strict orders that I rest until he gave the all clear and, anyhow, Divine D had told Mum that Hanaka's husband was the only visitor allowed at the hospital.

'Mrs Parker said the Japanese woman has had a breakdown, but physically she's going to be fine, and the baby too.'

Starting from the moment I'd noticed that strange other-worldly expression on Hanaka's face as Maggie shoved me into the car, and drawing on what I'd gleaned from my mother and from a girl at school whose aunt had once attempted to kill herself, as well as the innumerable novels that had come out of the Library Man's suitcases, I reconstructed the story of Hanaka's suicide attempt. In my story, Hanaka

177

turns away from the ugly scene of Maggie and me struggling; she walks into her house, her mother's white silk *kimono* slightly awry, locks the front door then calmly turns all the gas taps on the kitchen stove to full. Her face a parody of serenity, she opens the wooden chest with the crane lock and takes out the photograph of her mother and father, and two letters. Perhaps the smell of leaking gas is already apparent when Hanaka bows before her parents. In the bathroom, she removes a knife hidden inside a bag containing items from her trip to Sydney. Holding out one delicate wrist as if in supplication, Hanaka takes a deep breath and slices longways into the artery, bright blood pumping out from her, spilling onto the white silk *kimono* and the tiled bathroom floor. She imagines her father waiting. She sees dolphins playing in the sea of her homeland. Starting at the sound of banging on the front door, she thinks of the life inside her, but as Oldie shouts her name, she pushes the thought away and, quickly locking the bathroom, attempts to slice into her other wrist but she is trembling so much she fails to open the artery. Oldie is pushing at the door, shouting, and, after a slight pause, he rushes at the door which, on the second attempt, breaks open. Divine D is there too and both of them are kneeling on the bloody floor over the small broken figure, her face ghostly, her eyelids flicking open and shut, open and shut, as Oldie and Divine D fight to keep death at bay.

Each time I came to the end, my breath was almost gone and the pain in my chest made me worry that I too was dying. Over and over I repeated this scenario knowing that it was bad for me but unable to stop myself. I feared only a few small steps separated 'nervous exhaustion' from being declared to be mad.

2

But my family had no intention of letting me wallow, let alone go mad. One morning I awoke to Mum shepherding in Dr Martin.

'So, young lady, I hear you're feeling ... ' Dr Martin stopped for want of the right word.

'Time to get up, potter about, maybe help Mum, go for a walk. Fresh air, good food – all these will help, but you have to help yourself too. It's been a shock and I understand there's ... things you'll have to explain to your parents ... but Louise, you're young, you can put all this behind you ...'

This was the signal Grandma had been waiting for and, before I knew what was what, I was in the bath with her special lily-of-the-valley soap, then fully dressed and sitting in the kitchen with her and Mum. Dad was in bed, as he'd been on and off since being told Maggie wouldn't be coming back. Dr Martin killed two birds with one stone when he visited our house. He thought it time that Dad rallied too.

'Dad's still fretting about Maggie leaving but I've told him that if Maggie comes back, I'm going to Marlo with you two,' Mum said.

When had my mother got so ... so blunt, so plain speaking, so determined? Would she, could she, really leave my father?

'It's my fault,' I wailed.

'Stop feeling sorry for yourself, Miss,' Grandma said. 'If anything good is to come out of *your* mess, then this is it.

Uncle Tom's meeting Maggie and the solicitor tomorrow, and if she doesn't agree to selling Jack her share, I'll eat my hat.'

Although this was the first time Grandma had mentioned my 'mess' since she'd come to our house, whenever she looked at me her expression was an uncomfortable cross between mystification and annoyance.

I learned more about what had happened after Maggie dragged me home. When Mum had phoned the doctor she'd also phoned a hotel and a taxi for Maggie. Within an hour Maggie was gone. Mum staved off telling Dad what had happened until Grandma arrived.

One morning while I was eating breakfast Grandma fixed me with one of her looks. 'Fortunately, thanks to a friend of Oldie's, someone high up in the government, the police are turning a blind eye.' she said.

The police! I stood up, wild-eyed.

'What on earth's the matter, Lou?' Mum asked.

'Police! Did Maggie report me ...?'

'It's a crime to commit suicide. The woman is very lucky Oldie spoke to his friend or she might have been charged. Also with attempted murder.' Grandma said. Just to make sure I understood, she added, 'Attempted murder of the baby.'

Mum put her arm around me and changed the subject.

Almost every day, at least one visitor came to the house. Oldie called in most days, and Divine D came every second day, always with something delicious to eat. I'd lost weight but Divine D's 'temptations', as she named them, were doing the trick as my appetite slowly returned. Although Grandma and Divine D seemed to get on well, I sensed a reserve between them. When I asked Mum about it she said they were both women with strong views and in this case, different views.

'You mean, about Hanaka?' I asked.

'About you and the Japanese woman.' Mum answered.

Another regular visitor was Mum's Reverend Light who popped in and out of our house more frequently than I liked. I

180

couldn't bear it if he wanted to give me a little talk about sin and forgiveness. He never even tried – maybe he believed me beyond redemption – but he and Johnno seemed to have a lot to say to each other. Dorothy's Friends and their friends visited too, as well as Jenny and Libby, who looked very pale and unhappy. Even Dad's gardening boss came. Most surprising of all was Jonathan, who I wasn't up to seeing yet, but who wrote me letters full of fun and gossip with not one hint of what had gone on between us.

Johnno had somehow learned about Hanaka turning on the gas and he constantly asked me about it. I was glad he didn't know about the knife and the blood.

'Why did the Japanese lady want to make herself sick with the gas, Lou?'

'Unhappy,' I grunted.

'Aunt Maggie's unhappy. Is it the same kind, Lou? Will she turn on the gas too?'

'Aunt Maggie drinks.'

'She'd have to drink a lot for it to be like the gas, wouldn't she Lou?'

'More than an ocean,' I told him.

It was in another of Johnno's bulletins that he confessed he'd followed me to Hanaka's a few times and had gone there himself, once even into the backyard when no one was home.

'Aunt Maggie made me tell on you,' he said. 'Am I a traitor, Lou? She said if I didn't tell, you'd be sent away to a home for bad girls.'

'But then you told Oldie,' I said, 'and if you hadn't done that ... So really Johnno it was you who saved Hanaka. You're a hero!'

There was quite a silence while he took that in.

'Bye, Lou, I've got to go and help with tea.' His voice was very chipper.

It was also Johnno who asked the question that every member of my family wanted to know the answer to. 'Why, Lou? Why were you friends with the Japanese lady?' That

181

question was in my mother's concerned glances and my grandma's disapproving ones. If Dad had been up to it, his looks, I was sure, would be ones of total incomprehension.

But I was determined not to tell them anything. They'd never understand what Hanaka meant to me. No one had as yet spoken to me about her other than telling me that she was in hospital and would, in time, recover, and that she wouldn't be charged by the police. The very possibility of that happening made me so sad, that a person who was in such despair could be so punished. I couldn't help fearing that Mother McDonald might still do something even more awful but I couldn't even voice my anxiety about that to Divine D.

I'd come to the understanding that I'd done wrong in stealing from Maggie and lying to people who'd trusted me and that a reckoning awaited me. But it was the wrongs I'd done Hanaka that I regretted the most and I longed to see her in order to make those wrongs right. My family would never understand but as soon as Hanaka was well I was going to see her and beg her forgiveness.

So engrossed was I in my own drama that it took some time to realise that our visitors came not only out of concern for me, but also for the rest of my family. But I never even wondered why all these kind people were at my house rather than with Alan.

Whenever Divine D visited, she knitted as she talked, soothing me with the creation of a tiny matinee set in pale lemon which would do for either a girl or a boy baby, soothing me into believing that, in the end, everything would be alright.

3

My rehabilitation was considered complete when Libby and Jenny escorted me into town to see *Doctor in the House* and I returned to school a few days later. But the silence surrounding Hanaka remained. I'd convinced myself that Hanaka would forgive my deceptions and we would be even truer friends because, in the future, there would be no lies and no Maggie. If I kept silent until the time was ripe to see Hanaka and regain my relationship with her, I'd have the advantage over any family opposition because if Hanaka wanted to be my friend after all that had happened, some of it caused by me and my aunt, how could Mum and Grandma really object? Divine D, I was sure, had done a good job of explaining to my family about my friendship with Hanaka, although I doubted whether Grandma would ever be swayed. My family – Mum and Grandma at this point – because Dad was still in a bit of a state and so wasn't told much – didn't ever mention Hanaka because, I told myself, they feared talking about it would stir things up. They believed, least said, soonest mended, but they were wrong: as soon as Hanaka came home from hospital, I would go to her.

Grandma announced that Aunt Lily and Foolish were fretting for her, as was Uncle Tom, so it was time for her to return to Marlo.

'Well, Louise, I leave everything in better shape than it was when I first came,' she said. 'So let's have no more of your nonsense, young lady.'

'I'm sorry Grandma – I was wrong to steal. Mum's making me pay Maggie back £20.'

No matter that I'd be as old as Grandma by the time I paid off the debt and, if Oldie hadn't been given the maple tree and returned the money to me for Maggie, long dead.

'Not just the money and the lies, Louise, the woman, the Japanese woman ...'

'Hanaka. Her name's Hanaka, Grandma.'

'I don't care what her name is. You had no business being friends with her.'

'Why? Hanaka's lovely ... she's suffered too! I didn't think you were a hater like Maggie.'

'Don't be cheeky, Miss! I'm sure this ... Hanaka ... is a lovely woman even if she got herself into a terrible mess and tried to kill the baby ... But Louise, I can't forget that your father's life was ruined and, because of that, your mother's to some degree, not to mention the effect it's all had on Johnno with his asthma and his ... his worries.'

'That's so unfair! It's not Hanaka's fault!'

'Let me finish. I don't blame her personally, but I do say that your father suffered terribly fighting the Japanese. God knows what he went through and the final straw ... that poor boy, Danny ... beyond the pale ... way beyond!'

'What happened? Dad has nightmares ... but Mum won't tell me ...'

'It's too terrible ...' Grandma said. What could be so terrible that no one would even *say* it?

'From my point of view, Louise, it seems disloyal to your father, to his mates who died, to your family, including yourself, whose childhood as it should have been was taken away, to have a friendship with this woman. Do I make myself clear? Oh, before I forget ... ' Grandma handed me a book called *White Coolies*, which had a drawing on the dust jacket of a mean looking Japanese guard and women prisoners.

'To remind you of what some Australian nurses went through.' Grandma was, as I've said, a woman who spoke her mind.

❖

One warm November Saturday when summer was decidedly in the air Mum came briskly into my room and flung the window open letting in the scents of the garden.

'Up now, Miss. Oldie and Dorothy have come to see you. They're waiting in the garden ...'

Puzzling why, I called, 'Mum?' but my mother was already gone. I had a really horrible feeling ...

Divine D and Oldie were sitting under the lilly pilly tree at the table and chairs Oldie had made for us years ago.

'She's not ...?'

'Hanaka's coming along fine ... the baby too.' Divine D gave me some Castlemaine Rock and Oldie, a grave smile.

'We need to tell you about Hanaka,' Divine D said.

I put my hands up to cover my face but Oldie gently took them away.

'She'll get well ... in time ... as we've told you.' Divine D was looking at Oldie like a loon, who was looking back at her in the same manner. Were they both going senile?

'Alan's devastated,' Divine D added. 'It's been an awful awakening for him.' I felt a small cruel gladness at that.

'He didn't believe any of us at first ... not me anyhow, nor Naoko ... He blamed it all on your aunt ...'

'Me! It was my fault!'

'Girlie, that's real bull dust and ya know it.'

'I stole Maggie's money! If I hadn't Maggie wouldn't have come ...'

'Dear, you know Hanaka planned to end her life before your aunt ever came near the house. The letters ...' Divine D said.

In the letters, one to Alan, the other to Naoko, Hanaka nobly attributed no blame except to her own failings for which

185

she apologised. When Divine D spoke her mind to Alan about what had caused this awful thing to happen, she was vehemently disbelieved but Naoko summoned her husband to tell Alan the unpalatable truths about Mother McDonald. In Hanaka's letter to Naoko, she wrote that she was to be sent away, and that life for her child in Japan would be impossible. How terrible that life in Australia also had proved impossible for my beloved friend. Realising the truth, and full of guilt at his own blindness, Alan cut all ties with his mother, vowing in the future to devote himself to his wife's well-being. Although Alan had always failed to be the kind of hero I'd wanted him to be, I now realised he was a man who truly loved his wife and who'd suffered great losses because of that love.

Suddenly all my terrors burst from me: 'What if?' I whispered and tears came. Oldie moved to get out his handkerchief but Divine D beat him to it and hers smelt of lavender. What if, in that *split second,* I'd failed to understand the small clues and had not acted on my instincts? What if Oldie wasn't driving Pamela down the street because Johnno had told him about Maggie? It was the absolute stillness of Hanaka's figure in the front garden as Maggie struggled to get me into the car that had triggered the memory of Hanaka's words: 'I will leave him a gift.' In that smallest fragment of time my mind had summed up Hanaka's anguish and its sudden supposed resolution; her dream-like state of the last few weeks and that single word, leave – *she wants me to go away.*

'You're smart, Louise,' Oldie said. 'Smart in the head and smart in the heart.'

'*You* saved her life,' Divine D cut in. 'Harry and I believe that Hanaka will find both peace and contentment in the future.' Harry? Then I remembered that was Oldie's proper name!

Divine D looked at Oldie in a way that made me know they were going to tell me something else. With sudden clarity I knew it was something that had been kept from me.

'When will Hanaka be coming home?' I asked.

'She ... Hanaka isn't coming home here because ...'

186

'She's gone to Brisbane,' Oldie finished, 'Naoko is looking after her and when Hanaka's well enough ...' Divine D took my hand in her own.

'She'll come back?'

'No, Louise. Hanaka and Alan won't be coming back,' Divine D said, adding, unnecessarily as it happened, 'Ever. Alan wants them to have a completely fresh start.'

I'd cried then, sobs that wracked my body in the wretchedness of loss and regret and love. Oldie and Divine D tried to console me, later Mum and Johnno, even Dad. I didn't ask for Grandma's consolation, because I knew she'd be glad, and I couldn't forgive that, but she wrote me a lovely letter where she praised me for being such a good friend. Everyone told me, even Jenny and Libby, Jonathan too, that Hanaka would have a new beginning; she would have her baby and soon she would be well. But the ineradicable fact remained: Hanaka was gone from my life.

4

I grieved for weeks, casting a shadow over my family's emergence into sunlight, especially my mother, who for the first time ever was mistress of her own home. I'd written to Hanaka – five letters about six weeks apart. I never received an answer. The only person I ever spoke to about Hanaka was Divine D. She'd also written to Hanaka, and to Alan, a number of times, with the same result as me.

'Louise, I think we have to accept it, hard as that may be.'

'But I want to know that she's alright ... and about the baby ... and I want her to ...' I couldn't say the words.

'Forgive you? Of course she forgives you! What wrong did you do her? You were a good friend, and you saved her life. Hanaka will always know that.'

While I believed what I wanted from Hanaka was a final absolution, what I yearned for was rather different: to be sitting with *her* where we always sat, drinking lemonade and reading *The Weekly*. As I came to realise that neither of these things was going to happen, I trained myself to go for hours, then days, which slowly became weeks, without thinking of her, only to be suddenly thumped breathless by a sudden memory, an image. Sometimes I dreamt about her, dreams in which, wearing her mother's white silk *kimono*, she walked away from me into her house. Knowing what was going to happen, I knew I must save her but was unable to move. Another recurring dream was one where I was in a sublime Japanese garden desperately searching for Hanaka, but failing to find her. This dream, at first less ominous than the white *kimono* dream, still had the power to leave me raw and vulnerable.

Although I loved my family, in the time after Hanaka, it was a love in continual conflict with a need to be estranged from them, and such was my need to get away, I sometimes believed that if I didn't, I'd die. I became immensely independent, as self-contained as I could, never asking advice and very often contradicting my parents, which hurt them. It was only Johnno who I suffered any guilt about, and after brushing him off, or yelling at him, I'd always try to make amends by then spending time with him or buying him a bag of sweets.

'Mum said it's because you're a teenager,' Johnno told me once.

'What's because I'm a teenager?' I asked.

'That you're mean, and not like you used to be. When you stop being a teenager, Lou, will you go back to being how you were?'

Even in my fierce self-absorption, I couldn't help but feel shamed by my brother's words.

During this time my parents and Grandma had all become even more concerned about Johnno's attachment to his bower shelf and the ritualised way he played. As well, in the wake of the Hanaka mess, he'd developed a phobia about gas, checking and re-checking the gas jets before he'd go to sleep. One afternoon things came to a nasty head when he'd taken Paddy to see his bower. This had happened quite often before with no trouble as Paddy obeyed the rules that only Johnno was allowed to touch anything. Sometimes Paddy asked for a treasure to be moved, or to look at one more closely, and Johnno usually did so, but on this particular day a quarrel broke out over a battered miniature truck. Paddy, used to a more primal approach to disputes, swept the shelves of the old brown bookcase, causing Johnno's treasures to fall every which way. Johnno hit Paddy, who predictably hit him back, and by the time Mum got to the scene, it was on for

189

young and old. Their fight might have been seen as fairly inevitable, but not so Johnno's reaction afterwards. Sitting on the floor of his room amongst his disordered treasures, he rocked himself backwards and forwards, backwards and forwards. We tried to comfort him, but he wouldn't let any of us near him. When Mum suggested she pick up some of his treasures and put them back in the bookcase, he became so agitated we knew that things had gone way too far to be normal. Johnno fell asleep on the floor that night and we carried him to his bed. I slept in his room on an old mattress, watching over him as he had watched over me.

Next morning, Mum took him to Dr Martin who said Johnno had an anxiety condition and advised her to keep him in a calm, structured environment, and to keep him busy. 'He'll come right, if he isn't allowed time to obsess,' Dr Martin said. Rather similar to the belief that if a returned serviceman with psychological distress had a job which kept him busy, the man would stop obsessing, which in turn would lead him to eventually 'right' himself. My parents took Dr Martin's advice rather than seeking psychiatric help and, looking back, who could blame them, having been through the system themselves with its poorly trained psychiatrists, shock treatment without anaesthesia, not to mention the general lack of societal compassion for anyone suffering from a mental illness. Perhaps there were professionals who could have helped my brother, but I believe my parents couldn't face being exposed again to the humiliation that illness – and particularly, mental illness – brought with it. They'd had a gut-full: all they wanted was a relatively normal and quiet life.

Mum began to take Johnno to church, then he started going to Sunday school and, sometimes, much to my shock, Dad would accompany them to an evening service. I went to a few Sunday School concerts, one in which Johnno was dressed in a magnificent magpie costume, but I wouldn't go to church. As my parents banded together to give Johnno the stability they believed would do away with his anxieties, I became even more the outsider, the cuckoo in the nest, and

190

perhaps they were all waiting with bated breath for the day I'd fly away.

5

In time, and not such a long time either, I locked the memory of Hanaka into my deepest self, and turned resolutely to the task of growing up and becoming independent, and to expedite this growing-up, I threw myself into a flurry of sexual experimentation with Jonathan. As well, Libby and I hatched a plan to become nurses, and we chose a hospital which took trainees in when they reached seventeen, and where we would have to live in the Nurses' Home. This became my goal.

Only Johnno ever spoke of Hanaka, and that was mainly in the first few months following her disappearance from my life.

'I hope the Japanese lady is happy now, Lou. Do you think she is? Lou? Is she? Do you think?' I never answered him.

But the life force is stronger than the losses we suffer, especially when we're young, and by my final year at school I rarely thought of Hanaka, although I still dreamt of her on occasion. Mum had insisted that I stay at school to finish Form 5 before I started my training at the Austin Hospital. Why couldn't I leave school after Form 4, I'd railed, and take a temporary job in an office or a shop? But my mother, without Maggie to grind her down, and with the house now her own, was made of sterner stuff these days and stuck to her guns.

As my school years snail-paced their way to the end, I could hardly contain my excitement, although with freedom would come some losses: Jenny was going to train as a legal secretary, but at least I'd still be able to see her, but Jonathan was returning to England to go to University. 'Ah, well, Brat,' he said. 'We'll always remember each other, won't we? When I'm famous and write my autobiography, you'll be in it ... along with all the other women who come after.'

We were lying on his bed, reading a book from his parents' library about Rasputin, who was a crazed monk in the Tsar of Russia's court.

'You hope,' I said, 'But if you're going to write about sex, just call me "L".'

'Of course I'm going to write about sex! I want to make lots of money!'

'You'll have all these elegant French girls and ... and curvy Italian girls, and English girls, like the Queen ...'

'No! Not like the Queen, please, don't make me! Gina Lollobrigida ... now that's what I call a woman!' What was I? Though a different shape from Gina, I thought Jonathan liked my small breasts.

'Don't frown, Brat. You're as good as any of them. When you visit me in a few years time, I bet you'll be really beautiful.'

Perhaps it was that compliment, coming on top of what I took to be an unfavourable comparison with the Italian actress's breasts, that made me say, 'If ... if I couldn't possibly get pregnant ... If you could get one of those ... things that men ... I'd ... If you wanted to ...'

Jonathan was eager, but his task, rather like a prince with a quest to fulfil in order to win the princess, was difficult. The local chemist, the keeper of 'intimate' items such as condoms which were stored out of sight so as not to cause offence to other customers, was often as well an unofficial keeper of public morals. If a man asked a chemist for condoms, he would usually be given them, but if a *young* man asked, all he might get is a lecture and told to come back when he married. It turned out to be a hard and humiliating quest for what we'd nicknamed 'the holy grail', but Jonathan certainly tried: three chemists told him no, one adding that he should be ashamed of himself and another laughing at him. I think we were both going off the idea, I even toying with the possibility of Mum being right in her belief that 'a girl's virginity was a gift to her husband on their wedding night.' In which case, I'd have to get married very soon, because I wouldn't be able to wait long!

Then, suddenly, Jonathan triumphed! Where did he find the required, and, as I discovered, rather nasty smelling rubber necessity? In his own father's sock drawer. Soon after, I became a girl not able to give the gift my mother valued to any future husband. Knowing that, I felt a kind of defiant freedom, but sometimes I feared just how far away I'd moved from my family.

Two weeks before Christmas, and three days after my fifteenth birthday, Oldie and Divine D were married, and during the party afterwards – naturally, a garden party with many gardeners as guests as well as dogs, including Pep of course and Foolish and Tosser too – my mother said to me 'See, Lou, how you must take what you can from life and not be afraid.' Had she drunk too many shandies? I wondered.

'Both of them are old and maybe they won't have much time together, but they think it's worth it ... To love ...'

But my failed attempt to love and care for my friend Hanaka had left a bitter taste, and so I refused to understand what my mother was trying to tell me.

A wide river separated me from my family, a deceptively calm river which hid deadly currents, a river without boats, so even if I wanted to cross over to their side, I no longer could.

6

Finally I was free – and for the first three months, or more, was as frightened as the nurse my mother had so admired when she was ill. All day I ran up and down the long Thoracic ward carrying urinals, bedpans, sputum mugs and meal trays. Every morning I made more than twenty beds with another nurse who was three months ahead of me. At least a thousand times a day I answered Sister's call of 'Nurse Reid!' with 'Coming, Sister', 'Sorry, Sister', as well as witnessing for the first time a man's death, then being told to help lay his body out. Everyone was senior to me, and whenever I was spoken to I almost jumped, but it was the men who'd just returned from the operating theatre that day, after having a diseased lung removed, with tubes running from their chest cavity to a drainage bottle on the floor, an intravenous drip and an oxygen mask, who terrified me more than anything else. Even the old man with tertiary syphilis and T.B. who sometimes threw his dried-up faeces at the nurses was not quite as terrifying as these poor men, though I was always careful to approach him in a ready-to-duck combat position.

Libby, who'd started training before me and was now almost into her second year, helped smooth those difficult first months for me. Before long, the world outside receded and the hospital and the nurses' home became the real world. Young women hugely outnumbered men and every new resident doctor was scrutinised for the possibility that he might be romantic material, even if such a romance would be absolutely

195

forbidden! Still, gossips said, some girls did go up to the doctors' quarters, but they were senior nurses, or staff nurses who were already trained and, it was widely believed, those who did go, *did* stay overnight.

In my first year night-duty stint, which lasted fourteen weeks, I worked with a senior, Nurse Wilson, who told me she was shortly leaving the hospital. If it was quiet, we'd sit in the nurses' station and surreptitiously read magazines. Nurse Wilson always put her feet up on a chair, complaining about her swollen ankles. Sitting on Libby's bed one morning after breakfast, I learned that my senior was pregnant.

'Can't you tell?' Libby laughed at me. 'She must be at least four months.'

I asked Libby if a doctor was responsible, but she said if so he would have been able to get her a safe abortion, even though it was illegal. The thought of the alternative kind, which I'd read about in *Caddie*, when Caddie's friend Josie goes to a horrible, dirty room and a vicious old woman uses a piece of wire to induce her miscarriage, horrified me. I was also shocked that even a doctor, who surely wouldn't have been interrogated by a chemist, was so careless as to not use a condom. Libby and I discussed the possibility that the man was careless because he didn't give a hoot about the girl he slept with. Jonathan had given something of a hoot about me, which I'd have reason to recall in the future when I tangled with several men who didn't. Libby said that she wasn't ever going to be in that situation: that she was going to get married first. From this statement I gathered that Libby was still a virgin whereas I was not, but I never told her.

After that I watched Nurse Wilson very closely and even tried to turn the conversation to men and marriage, although I didn't quite have the nerve to introduce the topic of babies, but she remained as she'd been the previous seven weeks. Nurse Wilson's seemingly serene defiance of the rules of society, and of the hospital, made me greatly admire her.

How different this strange new world was from the world I'd left behind. At school we'd all straggled to our feet

196

when the Headmaster, Mr Cowan, came into the room, but as the most junior of juniors in the rigid hierarchy of the hospital, I was forever standing up or stepping back for almost everyone. If a consultant spoke to you, you were required to call him 'Sir' and although I didn't always like certain ward sisters, I respected them, and found it unpalatable to see such experienced women almost reverential in their encounters with Sir. I thought the ward sister and the consultant should be equals, even if it was the consultant who gave the orders on how treatment was to proceed, and the ward sister who saw that those orders were carried out. Libby called me bolshie, but I managed to get around that tricky word, Sir, by always calling a consultant by his name. On that long ago night when Bill had presented me with *Caddie* to read, Maggie's comment that he'd make a socialist of me yet, seemed to have gained some truth.

In order to be independent of my family, I'd entered this institution with its restrictive rules and regulations regarding my personal and working life. But at least I now earned my own wage and was even able to save toward a holiday at the end of the year; the institution fed me, cleaned my room and provided my uniform and, should I become ill, I would be cared for. Most of all, I was promised a future career which would enable me always to be independent, unlike my mother who had no training and had to take a job that paid very little and which was, she considered, a step down. The girl with the shocking-pink lipstick who'd worked at the local solicitor's might have had an air of doing exactly as she pleased, but I now knew that wasn't so. However, I was sure I'd taken a first step toward being a woman who might, in time, 'be free *sometimes* to do precisely as I liked'. As far as I was concerned, it wasn't such a bad exchange.

We had two days off duty each week, but if a lecture was scheduled on a day off, we were expected to attend it. At the beginning, I returned home on my days off and although I slept a lot of the time, I enjoyed the comforts and sounds of home around me, as well as the familiar depression of my body in the mattress. Mum would make a chocolate cake especially, and Johnno was always pleased to see me. I told them stories of favourite patients and ferocious ward sisters, and what I ate for breakfast, lunch and dinner, which held endless fascination for Johnno. I only told those things I believed suitable for my family to know. I didn't tell them about the woman who put a handkerchief over her face and wept when I assisted a senior nurse to dress the woman's ulcerating tumour which resulted from an undiagnosed breast cancer; nor the woman, not even forty, who had been lying for years in a box-like room of a dull grey colour with absolutely nothing pleasing or personal in it, and whose only movement was her eyes, even if that movement was involuntary; or the man who'd escaped the Nazis by hiding high up in the Tatry mountains of Poland, and who, on learning that his diagnosis was cancer of the lung, not the at first suspected tuberculosis, grabbed my hand and asked me if I believed in God. Sometimes Mum and I talked of the more serious things but she never pressed me for details. I think she was a little in awe of the work I was doing. I may have even believed that I now knew more about the business of life than my family did, except, probably Dad, but what I didn't know was that a chasm separated me, one amongst the well, from my father, one amongst the ill. However, I did gain a sense of how alone sick people felt, made much worse in those days by the absence of family involvement except at the scheduled and restrictive visiting hours.

After I'd been at the hospital for almost a year, I sometimes stayed in the nurses' home on days off and went out with one of my newer friends, or Jenny or Libby, if she was off duty too. Quite often I'd go on a blind date with a mate of Libby's current, and constantly changing, boyfriend. Libby never went too far with these boys but I found it very hard not to, and by the middle of the second year I had a boyfriend of sorts, best described as based on mutual convenience rather than true passion, and a relationship I kept secret from my family.

198

I never gave Maggie much of a thought, only when I came home and she wasn't there. So to be greeted with the news, 'Dad and I are going out to tea with Aunt Maggie tomorrow night,' from Johnno was almost like a smack in the face. Before my indignant response even had time to form itself into words, Mum silenced me with one of her newfound fierce looks.

'Johnno misses his aunt,' she stated. 'Dad does too.'

'Mum! Why?' I asked when Johnno was out of earshot.

'She's family,' Mum said.

'Not as far as I'm concerned,' I said.

'That may be so, Louise, but to Johnno and your father, she's very much a part of the family and they all want to put the past behind them.'

'What about you? I thought you hated her.'

'I've never hated Maggie. In fact, I've always felt rather sorry for her. You and she are the haters of the family.' Those words stung. 'Now that you've left home, I have to consider what Dad and Johnno need.'

I'd never fully realised that the space I'd left behind would inevitably be filled, but for it to be filled by Maggie reasserting herself as part of the family was infuriating. Although I'd longed to escape and had achieved my aim, I was strangely bereft at their ability to get along without me.

7

I'd made friends with several girls in my training group, but Libby was still my best friend. One night after we'd both finished our evening shift, Libby revealed the reason that she'd left her family and gone to her grandparents. Starting from the time she was twelve, her father had begun to make sexual advances toward her – at the beginning a hand that lingered on her blooming body in a place that may have once been acceptable but was no longer, repeated requests that she sit on his knee, persistently asking what she'd been doing if she went out somewhere, surprise openings of the bathroom door; finally, when he and she were alone in the house together, her father attempted to rape her, but she broke away from him and ran out into the street for safety. I was aghast. We were best friends and I hadn't even known. I'd kept secrets from her too, but the burden of hers must have been far heavier for Libby than my own.

Eventually Libby got up the courage to tell her mother a version that was damning, but not as shocking as the truth. Her hysterical mother told Libby that if she ever uttered one word of it to anyone, she would kill herself. 'I felt so helpless,' Libby said, weeping, as we sat together. 'My own mother wouldn't help me ... no one would believe me and I felt that somehow, it must be my fault ... something I did that was wrong.' Libby had nowhere to turn – her father's family would certainly disbelieve her, her mother's parents would die of shock, even an aunt she was close to couldn't possibly help her because of the conflict of loyalties and, yes, it was possible that her mother would make at least a half-hearted attempt at suicide. Such things simply didn't happen and, if they ever did, it was only amongst the poor, certainly never in a comfortably-off middle class family such as Libby's.

But Libby was a bright and brave girl – she went to the Salvation Army's headquarters and, after a few misunderstandings about whether she had run away from home, was led into a room where a pleasant looking grey-haired woman was going through files.

'I was afraid she wouldn't believe me, but she did. She asked me whether there was anywhere I could go and at first I thought no, but then I thought of Grandma and Grandpa. She suggested that I tell my mother it was either that, or running away, which would mean the police and probably everything coming out. "Remember, Anne," I hadn't told her my real name and she knew that, "you must be very strong and insist that you go to your grandparents. My guess is that your mother will agree and a cover-up will be concocted – go along with it – that's my practical advice, even though rightly the man should be punished. My dear, what's happened to you is not uncommon. Remember always, this is not your fault." By telling me that, she really saved me. When I'm rich I'm going to donate to them every year.'

Libby still occasionally met her mother and brothers for lunch at Buckley and Nunn, but she never visited her home. Her grandparents were kind and generous to her, if overprotective, and I can't believe they weren't aware of why she'd come to live with them, or at least had their suspicions, but as to whether they'd ever challenged their daughter or son-in-law, or instead took that over-worn 'least said, soonest mended' path, I don't know.

Six years later when Libby became engaged, yes, to a much coveted doctor, she told her father he was not welcome at her wedding, that she'd rather have the Devil himself escort her down the aisle. Not the Devil, but her grandfather did the

201

honours that happy day, as Jenny performed the duty of bridesmaid and I, matron-of-honour, both of us dolled up in aqua silk shantung. Eighteen months before I'd become pregnant, having lost the particular game of Russian roulette I was then playing, and married a boy who I never should have. Perhaps I was trying to emulate the seeming *sang-froid* of Nurse Wilson? My mother was terribly disappointed in me but the baby boy I gave birth to, named David, was a most beloved grandson. Although loving this child intensely, I knew already that I wouldn't stay with my husband. I knew too that freedom had slipped through my fingers. I could almost hear Grandma saying, 'Marry in haste, repent at leisure.'

8

As my life unfolded, the events of 1954 were largely banished from my conscious mind. Indeed, for several decades, if I'd been questioned about what had happened that year, and if it still pained me, I would have, almost truthfully, replied that I never thought of it any more. However, my unconscious had very different ideas, and the one dream – of searching for Hanaka – always recurred whenever I was worried or facing some sort of crisis in my life.

In this dream, Hanaka and I are in a garden, a Japanese landscape garden, but we are not together. Black pine trees grow on moss-covered hills with stones of different sizes and shapes arranged around them. Along the sides of the path I walk on, white camellias bloom, the fallen ones sprinkling the ground as if deliberately placed to enhance the scene. In the distance I can see a lake and, beyond it, a tea house, where I *know* Hanaka waits for me. I long to reach the lake, the tea house, to reach Hanaka, but the path twists and turns this way, then that way, becoming steeper and more treacherous with every step I take until I am stopped by a huge formation of rock blocking my way.

'Hanaka, Hanaka,' I call. 'Where are you?' Her laughter, light and playful, carries to me on the breeze. And then I wake up.

This dream always left me with a residue of sadness and regret, but two events, twenty years apart, gave it a far more powerful resonance. The first occurred when I'd gone to visit my parents with my little boy. At that time, I'd decided definitely to leave my husband and was worrying how I would both work and care for David who was not yet two years old. Johnno was still living at home and training to be an optician, but the day I visited he was working, as was Maggie. Yes, Maggie. More subdued, I was told, and less trouble, but still Maggie, back in her childhood home, living with my family as a boarder. We had an arrangement in which I only visited when Maggie was at work or, if she was at home, she'd go out when I came.

My mother knew I was unhappy and advised me to be patient, saying that marriages went through their hard times and that I was feeling like this at least partly because of the confines of motherhood after having been so free. I didn't have the heart to tell her I was already making my plans to go, that I simply could not envision spending my life with the man who not so very long before I'd promised to 'love honour and obey until death do us part', marrying him on the rebound from a love affair with someone who loved his freedom more than he loved me. To my mother and her generation, a divorcee was, if not exactly a loose woman, certainly a woman never to be trusted.

Oldie knocked on the back door and, seeing him standing there, older and frailer for sure, but still quintessential Oldie in his khaki overalls with a new Pepe de Moko at his side, made me lighter than I'd felt for some time. 'Ya Mum said ya'd be here this arvo, so I've come to take ya to Dottie. She's got a crook hip.'

It was not so much a request as an order, but as I hadn't seen Oldie or Divine D for almost a year, I gladly did exactly what he wanted.

'Better leave the little bloke with ya Mum. Not enough room in Pamela.'

Darling Divine looked older and frailer too, more so than Oldie, and there was something very serious in the way she greeted me.

'Sit down, dear,' Divine D said. 'We've got something to tell you.' I thought she was going to say that she was very ill. Oldie came back into the room carrying a tea tray. 'It came six months ago and, Girlie, ever since, we've been tossin' it backwards and forwards about tellin' ya or not,' he said, pouring the tea. I knew then what it was about. *Her* name stuck in my throat.

'A letter from Alan,' Divine said. Divine D pulled out a letter tucked down the side of the armchair she sat in. 'We were flabbergasted to get it. After all this time.'

I was more than flabbergasted: I was shaken.

'I'll read it, dear.'

5th April, 1964

Dear Mrs Parker,

I'm writing to you because my conscience has been at me for years but fear of the past has kept me from righting the wrong I've done you and all the others who showed kindness and friendship to Hanaka and who tried to warn me that things were not right.

The letters and presents people sent us were received but I never opened them until very recently as I couldn't bear to recall the day when I came close to losing Hanaka and our baby. She and I have agreed not to revisit this past, which you may not understand, but we were and are determined to make a clean break with what happened.

I am able to tell you that Hanaka is now well, although it did take a good five years and without our daughter, or Hanaka's friend, Naoko, I really don't know if it would have happened. We have a second daughter now and Hanaka is enjoying being the mother to our two girls that she was unable to be when our first was born.

When we'd decided to marry, I'd told Hanaka that I'd always look after her and if anyone or anything ever hurt her, they'd have me to answer to. That I failed

205

to live up to my promise weighs heavily on me, even today. In short, I was not up to the job. I brought Hanaka to live in Melbourne knowing full well that my mother would find it hard to accept our marriage. For a long time I blamed everyone and everything for what happened including you and the young girl Louise, whereas the fault was all mine because I could not face what was going on right before my eyes.

Please believe that we are both deeply grateful and our silence is only because it has been, and is still, too difficult for us to look back on that terrible time.

During the war, when I was in the Middle East, I hung on to the dream of returning home and settling down. That road has not been easy but we are making a life, a good life, and Hanaka has returned to her painting which brings her much ease.

Please think kindly of us and know that the friendship you gave Hanaka is remembered with gratitude. With belated but heartfelt thanks,

Yours sincerely,
Alan McDonald

Divine D handed me the letter and I clutched it to my chest as if it held the very essence of Hanaka herself.

'Dear, have we done the right thing? Should we have told you?'

I nodded yes through my tears, as joy and pain flooded me.

'He's a hero,' I at last managed.

'What, dear?' Divine D and Oldie were clearly puzzled.

'A hero. She deserved a hero,' I said, taking Oldie's proffered handkerchief and blowing my nose.

'You are a strange girl, Lou. People aren't characters in a novel whose story ends after two hundred pages. In real life, even heroes and heroines have to go on after their heroic act,' Divine D said.

'But that's what I mean about Alan. He'd always disappointed me but he's turned out to be a hero – not by

206

picking Hanaka up when she fell in the storm, then plying her with delicious food – by doing the really hard day-to-day things, and being patient and hopeful for the five years that it took for her to get well again.'

'Like ya Dad, too,' Oldie added. 'I reckon every day since his "heroic act" he's been a greater hero ... havin' to live with it ...'

'Poor Dad. He's pretty good now though. These new drugs ...'

'Ya Dad's better off havin' Maggie around too,' Oldie said. 'Even if most of us would prefer a good tar 'n' feathering.'

I was still clutching the letter.

'Now that we've told you, it's probably not a good idea to keep the letter.' Divine D said. 'We know Hanaka is well and happy. I'm so glad she's painting. That artist who gave her lessons believed she was very good.' Divine D put out her hand for the letter. The letter may not have held the essence of my friend but it was probably written in the house she lived in, resting on a desk or table she used, and by the hand she held which sometimes gently tucked a stray strand of her hair behind her ear: yes, written by the man she loved who had now surely shown that he loved her too.

'If you keep it, Louise,' Divine D said, 'it'll become a kind of holy relic.' She looked to Oldie to back her up.

'I don't reckon it'd be good for ya, Girlie.'

'The only reason we decided to tell you was that we thought having proof that Hanaka was alright was important. We know how much you missed her,' Divine D said.

I wanted to keep that letter forever as it was about as close as I was ever likely to get to her again. It *was* a holy relic.

'Burn it now,' I said. 'Please.'

Oldie put a match to the letter and placed the burning paper in the empty fireplace.

In the following months, I dreamt of searching for Hanaka in the garden three or four times a week and although the dream was the same, the feelings were sharper and more

207

desperate. Eventually I doused the dream with sleeping pills and my marriage break-up and the worries that came after, until it subsided into its vaguely disturbing version and mainly stayed that way.

The second event concerned my father and the long-held secret of the wartime experience which had made him mentally ill. In those days, the government only gave full pensions to men who could prove that the damage occurred directly *because* of the war experience, not *before* the war – in short, that they were mentally whole before active service and that it was the active service which had directly caused their mental health problems. How to prove this was well-nigh impossible. Added to this irony was the view that if one man saw the same service and coped, why should another man fall apart? Such punitive official views had no understanding that a man could be rendered mentally ill from the very act which had earned him a medal for bravery. Such was my father's situation. Over the years we forgot about his bravery, and his medal to prove it, because we, his family, lived with the contradiction of a hero whose heroic act was also the act which caused his ruin. At one stage when our finances were in crisis, my father apparently told my mother to pawn the medal, but she refused, and kept it in a safe place away from him.

What had happened in the war that made him cry like that? I'd asked this question many times, but never received a straightforward answer, only that what had happened was too terrible to speak of, that it concerned a young man called Danny who was a friend of my father's, and that this unspeakable incident was the reason my father became ill.

In his early seventies, my father was diagnosed with cancer of the lung and underwent basically the same operation as the men I'd been so afraid of when I'd first started my nursing training. He recovered from the operation but less than a year later developed secondary cancers and was dead within six months. It was only then that my mother told me what she knew. It happened in New Guinea where Dad was a sergeant. Dad became a sort of father-figure to an impetuous

208

bright-eyed boy of great charm, not yet twenty, called Danny, whose family had migrated from Ireland when he was a baby. My father tried hard to rein in the boy's impetuousness because sometimes it was dangerous, but Danny's charm always won him over. When their battalion was ambushed, Danny was shot, partly because he didn't immediately obey an order and partly because of the blackest of bad luck. That night, my father told my mother, the atmosphere in the camp was thick with a bitter sadness. Determined to retrieve Danny's body, my father volunteered to lead a fighting patrol the next day. They found Danny's corpse strung up and the flesh on his thighs and buttocks sliced off. On their way back to Base Camp they came under heavy fire from a Japanese patrol but, rather than abandon Danny's body, my father ordered the other men ahead with it whilst he held off the enemy, greatly endangering his own life. For this action, he was awarded a Distinguished Conduct Medal but, my mother said, all he felt was guilt that he had been unable to save his young friend, believing that if he'd been more impervious to Danny's charm and much firmer in tempering his impetuousness, this may not have happened. 'Of course your father had seen many terrible things, but what happened to Danny tipped him over,' my mother told me.

Although whispers of cannibalism by Japanese troops had filtered into the general population while the war was in progress and later, in the War Crimes trials, and because I was a child of a soldier who'd fought in New Guinea, that knowledge, along with other barbarous acts, surely lived at the edge of my consciousness, yet the reality of it never hit home hard until my mother told me this story. I was appalled, and in the weeks following my mother's revelation, when the dream of searching for Hanaka re-emerged, evoking in me such a longing to find her that I would wake with a heart heavy with yearning, I was also confused and conflicted. It was in the wake of this bewildering contradiction – my father's horrific experience in the Pacific War opposed to the snippets of knowledge that Hanaka had shown me, of Zen gardens, tea

209

ceremonies and Buddhist rituals which revealed sensibilities of the highest aesthetic and moral standards – that I began to read the history of Japan and of the Pacific War. By doing so I hoped to gain some kind of insight into this paradox.

I read of the battles for Papua and New Guinea, indeed, according to some sources, for Australia itself – an Australia left virtually undefended with the best troops in Africa and the Middle East. At the beginning, inexperienced and poorly trained Australian troops fought the Japanese in the most brutal of circumstances. The battle on the Kokoda track, where men from both armies faced an impossible terrain, moved me greatly. To be taken prisoner was considered dishonourable by the Japanese and they were expected to kill themselves with a grenade supplied for that purpose, indeed, often ordered by their superiors to do so. But during battle, grenades were often lost, and for many, while psychologically inured to death, their body's desire for life proved stronger. Through their leaders' arrogance, ineptitude, lack of understanding of the terrain and the monumental failure of adequate or even inadequate supplies, the Japanese soldier was left in this jungle to starve. 'Starve' – the word itself seems horrendously inadequate in describing the condition it is supposed to mirror – these men were *famished*, *ravenous*.

The truly hideous things in life are sometimes understandable: some are not. Whilst I reluctantly began to understand the act of cannibalism, I could never understand the cruelty that is attributed to the Japanese during this war. The closest I ever get to any comprehension was that Japan's feudal past and samurai tradition, so ingrained for so many centuries, asserted itself after the short time of Meiji democracy, but the code of honour of *Bushido* – the way of the warrior – didn't translate well into the accepted rules of engagement of 20th century warfare. No mercy was shown to soldiers on the other side and, soon, Australian soldiers, hardened by massacres and cannibalism, showed no mercy to the Japanese either.

210

Yet how to explain, or explain away, the reunion which took place in 1972 when eight survivors of the 39th battalion – militiamen of the Australian Army famed for their valour on the Kokoda track – travelled to Japan for a reunion with their Japanese counterparts? The Japanese sang their battle hymn and the Australians responded with *Waltzing Matilda*. 'Never could we find a time to outwit and outmanoeuvre the 39th,' an old general told the Australian reporter Alan Downer. 'We have waited 30 years to tell them so ... to tell them that our men of the great Nankai division ... thought they were facing an Australian Army some 10,000 strong on the Kokoda trail ... not ... just one battalion of young and untested men ... some 600 strong.' Was it the code of honour of *Bushido* that was well alive in this exchange, or was it a post-war moment of grace extracted from a landscape of horror?

My fervent hope when I was fourteen, of one day being able to read Japanese novels in translation, was, happily, fulfilled. *The Makioka Sisters*, translated and published in the United States in the late fifties was, just as Hanaka had said, a poignant story of a disappearing world – Japan before the Second World War. As for the Pacific War, Shohei Ooka, who was taken prisoner by the Americans in the Philippine defeat of 1945 and later became an eminent professor of French literature, wrote *Nobi* which was translated into English in 1957 as *Fires on the Plain*. It tells the harrowing story of the mental disintegration of a Japanese soldier who turns to cannibalism. Along with Norman Mailer's *The Naked and the Dead* which was translated into Japanese, and became one of the top-selling books there in 1954, it is considered one of the great anti-war novels of that time.

9

We're told nowadays that sixty is the new fifty, or even forty, but no amount of botox, gym work, positive thought, and all the rest of it, alters the fact that our biological design hasn't yet caught up with this trend. My career as a nurse over many years shaped and reinforced this view.

Surprisingly, I did have a Florence N vocation and became a ferocious ward sister and, as times changed and hospital structure became more egalitarian, later, a NUM (a nurse unit manager). I'd tried always to be fair to my staff and never *ever* used the word Sir to any consultant. My work gave me the structure and purpose often lacking in my personal world and my two children, David and Rebecca, were the glue that helped hold my life together.

My greatest heartache happened when I was in my early forties and Rebecca's father, my second husband, told me our marriage was over. I would have done anything to salvage it, and tried very hard, but it takes two to do so. I fell into a heap, drank too much and became unpleasantly bitter. It was my children who looked after me, when I should have been looking after them. Libby and Jenny were good friends to me during this time but it was my son, David, who finally told me a few brutal home truths – that I was a drunk, and nasty with it, and that I'd let myself go to shit. He'd help me clean up my act, but if I didn't, Rebecca would have to go and live with either him or Uncle Johnno.

'You're wallowing in it, Mum,' said David, who'd experienced two marriage break-ups, mine with his own father as well as his stepfather. 'It's pretty pathetic at your age.' His words acted like a ton of freezing water.

In time, and quite a long time too, I was glad that I'd loved so hard, even if I'd lost. But I never quite got over it. I had several other relationships which were mainly pleasant, but none that made me want to go down the marriage path again. The last, with a very nice man, interesting, thoughtful and an adept lover, came to an end when his later than mid-life crisis included returning to live in England. England is beautiful but I was not prepared to live away from my children and my city. We parted, saddened, but friends. There were still several men in my life who I could call on to accompany me to a party or the theatre and one in particular I shared with Jenny who is a widow. 'Is it okay if I have Robert on the 26th?' one of us would ask the other.

Whenever I found myself thinking, or worse, saying, such things as 'Public behaviour has gone downhill' or 'Surely I'm not the only woman in Melbourne who doesn't carry water wherever I go?' I'd raise my eyes to heaven and think how it would make my mother laugh to hear me. She'd been dead for almost ten years and I missed her. Often her words at Oldie and Divine D's wedding – 'See, Lou, how you must take what you can from life and not be afraid ... they think it's worth it ... To love ...' – came to mind, as did many of her sayings, and Grandma Henderson's too. Back then, I thought my mother knew nothing, understood nothing, but I was wrong. Had I taken what I could from life? Sometimes I thought I'd taken too much and not used it terribly well, at others, that I hadn't been brave enough to demand more. In this weighing up, I believed that about two times in four I'd fared pretty well and any regrets over the other two times were largely due to my own mistakes, and certainly weren't the 'slings and arrows of outrageous fortune' that can strike at random causing a life to be all but devastated. Although I'd raise my eyes heavenward whenever I thought of something my mother said, or believed,

213

my heaven-ward glance was both a gesture of affection as well as an ironic reference to her beliefs, because I remained a committed atheist, while Johnno became a practising Christian, fortunately one of the old breed, not the speaking in tongues variety.

As I aged, sex, regretfully, became largely confined to the imagination. Some believe there's no need for unwanted celibacy these days but it's the reality of many people's lives. What I really missed was sex as it once was – the ease and freedom and power my young body had given me. Occasionally, still, I became infatuated, usually with an oblivious man some years younger – but not *too* young: there's nothing like a schoolgirl crush to remind you that you're still alive. Hadn't I once scorned love in old age? Now I knew better!

My children were generous and loving, to their own credit, as well as believing, perhaps too much, in free and frank speech. My three grandchildren made me laugh as well as adore their small human perfection. I was healthy: I counted myself fortunate.

My mother and Grandma Henderson, along with my father and Uncle Tom, were buried in the Marlo cemetery. Johnno had wanted Maggie buried there too, but I put my foot down as she'd never been to Marlo and didn't belong there. She was buried next to her parents in the Melbourne General Cemetery. Johnno and I had managed to hang onto the Marlo house through various financial crises and we all used it for family holidays and time-out. The town still retained its small, secluded atmosphere and was blissful to visit in winter.

Johnno lived in a stylish flat in the centre of Melbourne filled with exquisite treasures from around the world. Although the same dear boy he'd always been, a great friend and a much loved uncle and great-uncle, Johnno had never managed a longstanding personal relationship, his one and

214

only fiancé breaking off the engagement after six months. We seemed to have that trait in common. He regularly saw a psychiatrist and took medication for his illness.

As for the dream, while such major events as my father's death and the break-down of my second marriage, exacerbated the dream of Hanaka, it always returned to its far less disturbing form. In a way, I'd become so used to the dream that its familiar story was almost welcome: the path, the black pines, white camellias, my heart beating in anticipation of seeing Hanaka in the tea house beyond the lake. Even when obstacles appeared and it became impossible for me to get to where Hanaka waited, sometimes my waking self was aware that soon I would hear her laughter and be glad that she was happy. It seemed that I'd managed to accommodate the dream into my life.

10

It turned out that I was wrong. As time went by, and despite the narrative remaining the same, the dream I'd believed accommodated became instead one where my longing to reach Hanaka, and my failure to do so, caused me such heartbreak that a residue of sadness pervaded my waking life. It was as if I was experiencing the very same heartbreak I'd felt at fourteen. I tried long, tiring walks, rational thinking, meditation, finally resorting to the occasional sleeping tablet which knocked me out and, although this left me dazed in the morning, it was better than the usual feeling of wretchedness. My doctor questioned my use of the sleeping tablets and said she wouldn't prescribe more. She suggested psychological help.

'This dream is clearly demanding your attention, don't you think?' she asked. It certainly was, but it seemed something of a failure to seek that kind of help at this stage of my life. My doctor disagreed. My stage of life, she said, was when many people had the need to understand the past.

After a month or so, I began therapy. My therapist, whose name was Judith Cavelli, said we'd be 'putting the files in order at the business end of life, and this file is the one marked "urgent".' I rather liked that description.

If, during therapy, the closely woven and intricate patchwork of my young life was slowly unpicked to reveal a girl made fearful too young of an unruly world in which she was powerless, a world which could take a man and, through no fault of his own, ruin him, it was also a liberating experience to at last speak of Hanaka, our meeting, the parsley sauce-making and Hanaka's triumph when Mother McDonald praised it after being told the lie that a neighbour had made it, and the sweet friendship we developed as we read magazines trying to find out how to become what society expected of us – Hanaka, to turn herself into an Australian housewife, and me, an Australian young woman who was expected to become an exemplary housewife. One of *The Women's Weekly* covers of 1954 showed an attractive woman, wearing a full skirt and blouse, flat shoes, hoop earrings and a kerchief tied into a cute knot on the top of her head. The caption read: 'Glamour in the Kitchen'. While we might have conceded the possibility of the kitchen giving us pleasure in cooking delicious foods, neither of us could really see it as anything other than duty (Hanaka) or drudgery (me) which left me, at least, wondering where on earth I could fit in. Thank goodness we had other sources at hand. It was the books we read and talked about together that taught us, even if we didn't realise it then, about other kinds of women, women who had found it necessary, even essential, to live in ways that society didn't always accept. Even with the pain another way of living often brought with it, I was glad I'd failed to live up to that comfortable but restrictive middle-class archetype of 'Glamour in the Kitchen'. I wished with all my heart that Hanaka too might have found a way of living that was true to herself.

'Your father, Jack,' Judith asked in one early session. 'You were fourteen, that's right isn't it, when these events took place? Can you recall how you felt about him at that time?'

'I remember being terribly conflicted ...'

'In what way?'

'To start with, he was often what kids would call a loony. But we hid that as much as we could from the world –

which meant the neighbours and mothers of other kids – but they all knew something wasn't right , so I often hated him.'

'It's not uncommon to feel this, especially when the father is not what the child wants him to be.'

'I remember when I was younger looking at the photo of him in his army uniform and wishing so hard for him to be like that again. I got to hate that photo. I'd turn it to the wall, but after a few days it would be turned back the right way.'

'Were you ever afraid of him?'

'When he was drinking and raving, yes. Once he came into the kitchen without any clothes on ... I was about eleven and it really frightened me ... It was the first time I'd seen a man naked.'

'What did you do?'

'Ran out of the room shouting for Mum.'

'Almost any young girl confronted by her father's nakedness would be appalled and frightened. Adults forget how modest young people are. Yes, even the ones who wear what we think of as barely covering them. I was very surprised when my fifteen-year-old daughter refused to let the cat into the bathroom because we'd belatedly realised the cat was a he and not the she who was allowed to sit on the edge of the bath and watch the water.'

This little anecdote made Judith seem more human and lightened the burden of the telling for me.

'How did your mother handle the situation?'

'She was very gentle with him – led him back to the bedroom, helped him dress, I suppose, because the next time I saw him he was dressed.'

'But what about you? How did your mother handle you?'

'Mum said he meant no harm and was sorry. He was depressed, she said. As if I didn't know that.'

'How did that make you feel?'

'Guilty.'

'Why, guilty? You did nothing wrong.'

'Because I felt ... resentful ... resentful about ... everything in our situation.'

'I would imagine your resentment was more personalised. Weren't you angry? With your father?'

'Sometimes I hated him, as I said, and wished he'd never come back from the war ... then I'd feel guilty because it wasn't his fault.'

'So you couldn't be angry with your father. What about with your mother?'

'None of it was her fault.'

'So you had no one to blame for your anger and, from what you've told me, no one you could tell how angry you were. How awful ... Apart from feeling guilty because you were angry at what you call "your situation" you must have felt very alone ...'

'I've never thought of it as feeling alone but, yes, that's what this feeling of never ... never being given what I needed. Not being able to demand what I needed.'

'You're entitled to feel anger and resentment, but, as you know, somewhere along the line it would be good if you could find a place to blend it in – a bit like when you cream together butter and sugar and must then mix the eggs in. You know what happens if you do it too quickly? We don't want curdled ... ' We both laughed.

11

Through therapy, I came to accept emotionally that I wasn't to blame for either Hanaka's treatment by her mother-in-law or her breakdown. And if, in the end, I still didn't quite see myself as any kind of heroine, I could acknowledge that my motives in befriending Hanaka, though not without convolutions, were largely to do with an irresistible longing to know someone who was noble, kind and beautiful enough to answer my need for a true heroine. Not someone I read about in a book, but a flesh and blood heroine who I could learn from. It's hardly surprising that with my taste for drama, and being spellbound by difference, that heroine would come from a background totally alien to mine.

Hanaka and I had debated whether Melanie Wilkes or Scarlett O'Hara was the greater heroine, and while I defended Scarlett for her tenacity and desire for survival, Hanaka believed she was selfish and unkind, and that Melanie was a far worthier heroine, exhibiting all the finest and strongest of womanly virtues. Back then, Anna Karenina had presented us with quite a dilemma, as she was not how we understood a heroine to be – dead on a railway track. One needs age, experience and compassion to fully understand Anna. Most importantly, in the wake of what happened when I was fourteen, I'd learned the hard lesson that flesh and blood heroines and heroes never have the neat all-ends-tied-up endings that fictional ones do, and that men and women –

such as my father and mother and Hanaka and Alan – prove their true worth in the aftermath of the drama.

The convolutions in my motives for befriending Hanaka were to do with my choice of heroine, a woman who represented the shadow side of my father's – and family's – pain. Perhaps my initial determination to make contact with Hanaka had to do with a dark compulsion to know that enemy; perhaps it was about rebelling against the reality of what I'd lost in my young life because of my father's illness.

The most important understanding I came to was that because of my father's psychological war damage, and my mother's earlier depression, I'd made myself the parent, taking on a responsibility which was not and should never have been mine, for keeping things right. And when my efforts failed, either because of the conduct of others or my own, which swung wildly between irresponsible and over-responsible, I was left with both anxiety and guilt – and anger.

For me, the loss of not having a 'whole' father, and the anxiety of his illness during my entire childhood was compounded by the nature of the ending of my friendship with Hanaka, causing me excessive grief. Or was it excessive? After all, a person I loved had tried to kill herself following a violent situation with my own aunt. Add to that my total loss of that loved one and the tearing of my fragile family group, even if at the time it was necessary, and I was glad. Nevertheless, it was a very unhappy experience for all involved. That fourteen-year-old girl, thus wounded, still whispered inside me, bypassing all logic and evidence, and had not been stilled as I marched toward old age. Once, in therapy, I'd shouted, 'She wasn't crippled! Why couldn't she contact me? I really needed that!'

'Wasn't she? Perhaps not physically, but from what you've told me, she was brought undone and was seriously ill,' Judith answered. I began to cry and she handed me some tissues.

'You know, Louise, to come back from that kind of breakdown in those years, long before the generation of drugs we now have, is quite remarkable ... if the husband was telling the truth in the letter you told me about ...'

'She painted ... He said in the letter it brought her ease. I was the one who encouraged that ... He didn't want her to ...'

'Imagine what it must have been like for him. But he didn't abandon her, and you know as well as I that people abandon people when there's illness, particularly mental illness.'

'My mother didn't abandon my father.'

'Was she right?'

'Then, sometimes, I thought she should, but now ... now I'm glad she didn't ...'

'Why?'

'Because he's my father and ... and it wasn't his fault! I'm proud of him.'

'In what way proud?'

'He fought a war for his country, a war that cost him dearly. His life and my mother's would have been so different if he hadn't fought. And he tried to get well again but it was really hard.'

'So, Louise, can you forgive your father for what he couldn't give you?' Judith asked.

12

Through the examining of the events of 1954, I also began to remember the girl I once was, but in a different way, a way that was full of something like wonder. I'd been such a wilful and resilient wisp of a thing with such a fierce determination to challenge the malevolent Fates who spun out the thread of a life, followed its course, and directed the consequences of actions according to the counsel of the gods; to reject their power to cause a man to become another man, a fearful tormented man. I applauded this girl's courage; I laughed at her deeds and misdeeds and was moved by her self-doubts. With something like envy, I remembered her head-long dive into love and sex and that first rather sophisticated yet amazingly guileless encounter with the charmingly precocious Jonathan. I hoped like mad he hadn't become a boring old fart. I began to cherish the girl I'd been and, finally, in understanding that that girl was still within me, I began to see my life more in terms of triumph than hard-won contentment amongst many losses. In re-thinking this wild, complicated, funny girl, I rediscovered that a life-force was still well alight in the pleasure I found in small things, rather than the large; the shimmering yellow glaze on a 1930s vase; prunus blossom, the first sign of spring in a dreary Melbourne August; a pair of ruby-coloured shoes, this time with diamantes instead of bows; the taste of an early morning cup of tea sipped from a hundred-year-old English china cup and the wonder of its history and survival.

But while my sixty-seven-year-old head understood that an imperfect end to the story of my friendship with Hanaka was the reality, the dream continued even as therapy brought me much ease. Judith thought I might be able to master the dream by thinking of its better aspects: the Japanese garden in all its magnificence, and especially the sound of Hanaka's carefree, girlish laughter. Also, with perseverance, I could teach myself to wake up during the dream. When this happened, Judith instructed me, I should listen to music for half an hour before going back to sleep.

David set me up with an iPod loaded with music. I chose *Pictures at an Exhibition*, a suite of ten piano pieces composed by Modest Mussorgsky to depict a tour of an art exhibition – paintings by his artist friend – to be my companion in the night. As well, before sleeping, I'd spend ten or so minutes recalling a particular time with Hanaka, a good time, firmly keeping other memories at bay.

Although many people today believe in closure as an almost automatic occurrence or 'right', I believe grief to be its own master with its own path, its own time frame. Harm is done when people believe that by performing this ceremony, or by passing that milestone, they can forever put their sorrow away – the best that is often possible is finding a place that is bearable. Because of the grief the dream of Hanaka brought me, I knew that I hadn't found such a place for my long-held sadness. That was why I'd commenced therapy. While not expecting closure, I was hoping to achieve a kind of truce with my unconscious.

❖

'You said, "I wanted to say goodbye. I wanted to tell Hanaka how much she meant to me." Didn't you want something more?' Judith asked me one Monday morning.

'What do you mean?'

'What was it *you* wanted? What didn't she give *you*?'

'I wanted to say goodbye. Why couldn't she have let me? I wanted ... her to ....'

'Find the words, Louise.'

'I wanted ... wanted her to tell me how much ... she cared ... how much *I* meant to her ... but she never did ... although the letter from Alan explained it.'

'Are you angry?'

'No! How can I be angry with her? It wasn't her fault,' I began to weep.

'You're entitled to be angry, Louise.'

'I don't want to be! I hate this! I want it to stop!'

'I believe you need to acknowledge it ... feel it ... '

'Maybe she hated me ... ' That possibility, that fear, cut deep even after more than fifty years.

'That's you at fourteen talking. What would you say now?' Judith asked.

'That ... she ... Hanaka had to concentrate every ounce of her being in order to survive.'

We sat in silence for a few moments while I wiped my eyes and blew my nose.

'Louise, it seems to me that your adult self knows that it's not possible for Hanaka to give you what you want, but your fourteen-year-old-self has trouble accepting this. Do you think that's so?'

'Yes, but how do I ... ?'

'Have you ever thought about going to Japan? Often the things we fear – and you still do fear Japan – are those we need to go out and greet. It may help you to accept what you can never have.'

225

Later that day, thinking back on the morning's session as well as Judith's out-of-the-blue suggestion about going to Japan, I opened the doors that led to my small walled garden. When had the jasmine started to bloom? How could I not have noticed this harbinger of the end of winter? I breathed its heady sweetness and suddenly thought of Grandma Henderson and her odd gift. What conclusion would she have come to about my home? I went back inside and sniffed but, apart from dust, I couldn't smell anything except staleness. Staleness smells as if something essential is absent, missing. If I'd possessed my grandmother's gift, what I'd smell in my home would be an alarming *lack* – a lack of vitality, a lack of caring enough, a lack of the courage necessary to engage fully with the world. A lack of *curiosity*. When had this happened?

Every suggestion of Judith's so far – and she'd given me plenty to keep me busy – always turned up something worthwhile to think about. Her suggestion that I go to Japan was no exception. I said the words in my head. Then I repeated them out aloud. *I am going to Japan.* I felt almost light-headed.

13

Afraid of being adrift and alone in Japan, I persuaded Jenny to come with me on a Cultural and Garden tour. A tour has boundaries, strict departures and arrival times, meals, luggage and all the rest taken care of, and Jenny was, as she said herself, a perfect chaperone. After the tour ended we were going to travel by ourselves, telling each other that by then we'd have the hang of it.

On arriving at Kansai airport, my first truly Japanese moment came as the airport bus pulled away and all the luggage attendants, standing in a row, bowed to it. In Kyoto we watched as a *maiko* – an apprentice *geisha* – on her way to an early evening appointment, was forced to break into an oddly comic run in order to escape a pursuing pack of camera wielding tourists. At the Fushimi Inari shrine with its famous avenue of *torii* gates which we visited in the late afternoon, the fox statues added such an eerie feel that I could almost sense the presence of the spirits of these animals, said to be able to inhabit a human – even though I absolutely *don't* believe in such things. Jenny said it gave her the creeps. After the tour ended we were on our own, except for the endless help given to us by railway and hotel staff, and by perfect strangers. Our night at a *ryokan* – where, shortly after arrival, the wind began roaring, the noise like a train coming through the wooden building which began to shake as did the vase on a low table as we too wobbled precariously and the girl who'd brought us

227

green tea looked plain terrified – was exhilarating *after* the earthquake had stopped. In Osaka a woman taxi driver had trouble finding the Museum of Ceramics, and as we drove from place to place searching, she and Jenny ended up singing *Sakura, sakura* (the cherry blossom song), much to my almost-embarrassment, until I relaxed and enjoyed this good-natured sharing between two people with few words in common. Jenny said later that she knew only the one word, *Sakura*, but made up for that by humming.

Journeying in a bullet train so clean that one could have eaten one's dinner from the floor and where the ticket collector bowed to the passengers on entering and leaving the car, the ugly landscape of crowded unattractive buildings and myriad overhead power lines gave way to more rural landscapes as we crossed from Honshu into Kyushu, and then sped beside the sea in a local train to Nagasaki. This city with its history of Portuguese and Dutch traders, of Jesuit missionaries, as well as its close ties with China and Korea, was where the Americans dropped the second atomic bomb, named Fat Man, on the industrial centre on August 9th, 1945, a bomb more powerful than the one which had destroyed Hiroshima three days earlier. At the epicentre of the blast is a huge black memorial stone with gold lettering. While sobering, it didn't prepare me for the memorial museum, especially the minutiae of the disaster such as the bones of a hand burnt into melted glass, or a photograph of black stiffened corpses reminding me of cattle after a bush fire. But most sobering of all were the many people of my age, and older, who I walked past at every corner, in every arcade, up every pretty, hilly street; people who had been *here then*. I wouldn't have been surprised if I'd been spat on; I would have been upset, but not outraged. No, the outrage would clearly not be mine to claim. Our visit passed without such an incident. Instead, once when we were lost, two schoolgirls – rather plain, plump girls about fifteen – escorted us in the pouring rain, shielding us with their one slightly broken umbrella, to where we wished to go,

228

protesting all the time that they were going the same way. Yet, when we left them, they turned back to where we'd come from.

Did I glimpse her? Did I sense her? Everywhere *something* reminded me of Hanaka: the back of a woman's neck, the way a woman smiled, the *kimono* shops stocked with a huge array of *kimonos* and where, once as I stroked one of these glorious things, I could almost feel the softness of her skin underneath the silk. When we were buying handkerchiefs for gifts – found in every department store and even made for the Japanese market by European fashion houses because *every* Japanese woman carries one for wiping hands, or using as a serviette when eating lunch but never, *never,* for blowing noses – I asked an assistant what the Japanese name for them was. She turned to her friend and consulted, then laughingly replied, 'Han-ker-chief!' Her gesture was so like Hanaka's – her small, perfect hand held over her laughing mouth – that it transfixed me for a moment.

I stopped for a day in Kure, not far from the city of Hiroshima, and situated in a natural harbour on the Inland Sea surrounded by mountains. Jenny went on to Himeji where we would meet up later. Kure was where the Australian contingent of the British Commonwealth Occupation Forces had been based after the war and where Hanaka worked and met her future husband. I didn't know the name of the town outside Kure where Hanaka once lived with her aunt and two cousins and, anyway, many of these small towns were now amalgamated into the city. Wanting to walk some kind of path to honour my lost friend, I took a train, getting off about half an hour from the city centre. I walked the streets of this unknown neighbourhood, past a market selling bonsai, azaleas, second-hand *kimonos* and books. It was a small-town place with none of the splendour of Kyoto, a place of modest homes replete with potted plants, small dogs and street shoes on doorsteps, unlocked bicycles parked outside. Later I took the short boat trip to the island of Etajima, also used by the Australian Occupation Forces. Hanaka once told me this was where she and Alan had picnicked one spring and as they sat under the flowering cherry trees, dolphins played in the sea.

When we visited the Kenroku-en gardens in the city of Kanazawa, whose landscape was similar to my dream, I caught a glimpse of Hanaka on a path, crossing over a wooden bridge, then waving to me from a tea house. But this was only a feverish kind of imagining of another outcome to my troubled dream.

The grand avenue up to the Meiji shrine in Tokyo is lined by trees and surrounded by acres of garden with impressive red *torii* gates across the path to remind you of the sacredness of what you are walking toward. What I hadn't even thought about was that this shrine was a popular place for people to marry according to Shinto rites. Slightly disturbed to see so many brides, splendid in white *kimonos* lined with red silk, their grooms in dark ones, I forced myself to remain in the moment because the last time I'd seen such a wedding *kimono* had been on the day I'd last seen Hanaka.

One after one the couples came into the courtyard led by a Shinto priest in platform shoes followed by young girl attendants attached to the shrine and then the family members of the bride and groom. It was the end of the ceremony, I realised, because people began taking photos and the solemnity gave way to happy smiles. When, as another procession came into view, I saw that the bride was Japanese, but the groom, European, the lump in my throat became tears. Weddings don't usually make me cry but this wedding of two strangers from two different worlds did, and I couldn't stop. I was very glad of my 'han-ker-chief' and my friend.

Despite being very aware of being in Hanaka's homeland, my trip to Japan didn't, of course, turn up any miraculous closure, but I wasn't expecting it to. Before I'd left, Judith told me to regard it as a kind of staging post in my quest to understand the past. Yet I did learn a number of invaluable lessons. One was that the knowledge Hanaka had given me so long ago of a Japan unlike that of wartime Japan was a gift. It had enabled me – even with my father as he was – to

230

understand that although a country's wartime action comes out of its very culture, it is only a part of that culture taken to toxic extremes. Hanaka – by simply being herself – had shown me the existence of another Japan, a dazzling place, not the dark hell which the Showa period brought to the world as well as to its own people. The other lesson was to do with curiosity. And its lack. My journey to Japan had been fuelled more by bravado and need than curiosity but once there my curiosity went into overdrive. The priceless souvenir I returned home with was my re-awakening of *the desire to know*.

This awakening led to a number of sessions with Judith, appraising my life as it was now and the need for me to make sure my curiosity was kept well alight. We discussed ageing and what has been described as 'when the centre starts to drift away'– when the world becomes just too bewildering and goes speeding past – which does happen with old age.

'But I'm not anywhere near that yet,' I told Judith. 'I'm going to be *here* for as long as possible.'

'Perhaps you need to connect more ... '

I told Judith of my previous foray into joining a book group and my early argument with an established member.

'She was dismissive of any illness, considering her own good health a sign of her moral superiority. I almost wished her an awful disease. Then she'd learn what endurance and courage were all about! '

'You feel strongly about this ... What did you say to her?' Judith asked.

'That it was mostly down to genes and luck and to suggest otherwise was plain ignorance. It did not go down well.'

'Maybe you tried to join the wrong book group. Indeed, I'd go so far as to say, perhaps a book group isn't for you. You're something of a ... '

'Bolshie? My friend Libby still calls me that.'

'I was going to say an outsider. But all groups have rules – often unspoken – that members must conform to. I

231

don't think you're always prepared to do that. If you want to connect you may have to flex more ... '

'I'd like to have some young people around me – not too young but younger than me – rather than a bunch of women just like me, with our opinions stiffened by years of giving them to all and sundry ... '

Judith laughed out aloud. 'Does that include yourself?'

'I fear it does. And I'm bored with myself.'

'Be aware of new ideas, new possibilities. Do something you've never done before. Challenge your own world view. But most of all remain open to the *desire to know*.'

'First I'm going to fix my house up,' I said. 'Get it painted, new bookshelves, big windows, a dishwasher that works properly and a new bathroom. Then buy some original art works – down Marlo way there's quite a few good landscape painters.' This thought was a fairly new one and it reminded me of that small watercolour Hanaka had given me of how our garden was to be: I'd stored away the watercolour more than thirty years ago yet I still knew exactly in which box it was stored. I would have it framed and placed where I could see it every day.

So it went for a few more sessions until at last I felt able to say to Judith that we seemed to have come to the end.

'What makes you believe that?' she asked.

'The dream is under control, more or less, and I can live with it now. What I needed to do was to unburden, and then try to understand what had happened, and why I'd reacted as I did.'

'Do you feel as if you've found a place for your pain?'

'It certainly has eased. If, sometimes, I have to move the pain from one place to another, somewhere, as you said, it blended in better, I believe I could do that now.'

'That's a good place to end then,' Judith said.

I gave her a gift from Japan: a small *sake* cup of exquisite beauty. Gold leaf decorated the inside and, on the outside, over a grey-green base, the artist had painted, in delicate brush-strokes, darker green hill-tops all around the cup, the grey-green base creating the illusion of mist on foothills, foothills which in fact did not exist. Judith hugged me. Later, I sometimes imagined the *sake* cup to be on her desk, or somewhere in her home, and when she glanced at it, perhaps even picked it up, she would remember the journey I took with her.

Through the intervention of an acquaintance known to the employer, I got a Sunday job in a bookshop – no need to join a book group as all the staff, and many customers too, had vigorous *opinionated* views on the books they read. Opinionated views I had to listen to: views I began to *learn* how to listen to, rather than dismiss out of hand. I also became a guide at the National Gallery of Victoria. My first time with a group before Mark Rothko's *no 36 red* was terrifying because not so long before I too had gazed at this painting with both the incomprehension and apprehension I saw on most faces in the group. My challenge became to have that fear and blankness give way to a gleam of understanding and the pride that brought to the viewer. Of course in every group there were always one or two who began with contempt in their eyes, the ones closed off from the desire to know.

As for the dream, it continued, but in a much milder form. I still used the strategy Judith had shown me. But occasionally I'd let the dream run its course so I could hear, once more, Hanaka's light and playful laughter. I may never have mastered the dream, but never again has it mastered me.

14

More than two years after I'd finished therapy, I received a note from Judith enclosing a cutting from a Brisbane newspaper dated the week before. I read the note before I unfolded the cutting. Judith wrote that she'd come across the article when she was up there attending a conference and felt strongly that she should pass it on to me. She also wrote that I could ring her if I wished to. I unfolded the cutting and came face to face with the same photo of Hanaka and Alan on their wedding day that had been in their lounge-room. Another photo showed two middle-aged women standing in front of several paintings. They were, I read with a racing heart, Hanaka's daughters. The blood pounded in my ears as I scanned the article: Hanaka was dead. She had died five years before and the article was about a retrospective exhibition of her painting being held in a Brisbane gallery.

My first reaction was, no, no, no! But having read the article, it was too late. This unwanted and unlooked-for knowledge completely unnerved me. What would it do to my hard-fought efforts to have the past reside somewhere within me that was not too painful? I threw the newspaper cutting into the rubbish, determined to ignore what it contained. But a deep longing held tightly in my very soul for decades was awakened, and after a night of dreaming I knew I must go and see Hanaka's paintings.

On a Brisbane winter day of perfect blue sky and a temperature of twenty-one degrees, I walked into the gallery showing Hanaka's work. I took a catalogue from a stylish woman whom I took to be the owner of the gallery, and from then on I was lost to this world.

After recovering from a nervous breakdown she suffered during her early years in Melbourne, I read, Hanaka McDonald took up painting again. Over the next twenty years she gained a reputation for her finely wrought and sympathetic studies of the natural world which contain a stunning cohesion of both Western and Japanese influences. During her final two decades her work became more abstract and this work is now considered her finest, especially in her native Japan. I couldn't have been more awestruck if I'd wandered without prior knowledge into *Saint Chappelle*. It was me who'd encouraged Hanaka to paint, who'd witnessed her first careful strokes of watercolour even if later I was to be jealous of her devotion to it. After her tragedy I had no doubt that this ability to paint helped to make her well again.

The catalogue listed an impressive number of galleries which owned her work and on the last page was a biography citing her birth, her marriage to an Australian serviceman, her nervous breakdown and the birth of her first daughter, Naoko, and four years later, her second, Takara. She and her husband and children had then returned to Japan, where they'd lived for several years before coming back and settling permanently in Brisbane. Over the page was the shock of a wonderful photo of Hanaka when she was an old woman. Suddenly faint, I looked around for somewhere to sit. The gallery owner was quickly by my side with a chair. 'I'll get you a glass of water,' she said.

Sipping the water, I told this woman that I'd known Hanaka – 'When I was a young girl,' I said. She told me how moving the opening of the exhibition had been. Hanaka's husband and daughters and their families and an old lady, who the gallery owner took to be Hanaka's sister, had all been there. I thought it must have been Naoko.

235

'Her husband was so proud of her,' the woman said. 'It was a strange occasion, very sad but also happy. Usually, of course, openings are all about posturing, ego and money.'
She then brought me a cup of tea with two sweet biscuits on the saucer.

'Eat them,' she commanded and I did so as I'd hardly had any breakfast before catching the plane.

Energised once more, I began to view the watercolours but the excitement and elation I'd felt from the time I'd walked into the gallery abruptly gave way to a stunning reversal. What was I doing here? It was all far too much – far too late. It would have been better not to have come, better not to have known, not to have known ... her? No. Not for anything would I ever wish that. Tears brimmed and I turned into a side alcove to wipe my eyes. In this alcove hung two smaller works with a larger one between them and, in order to gain control of myself, I turned to the larger work.

Was I going to need another chair? The watercolour was full of images, utterly familiar. I took a deep breath. Before me lay a Japanese garden enclosed by bamboo fencing, a white camellia tree on one side and a stone lantern at the beginning of a path with azaleas on both sides leading to a small rock-strewn hill where a perfect maple tree grew. The entire background was taken up by a huge tree glorying in its new blossoms, patches of an old weatherboard fence showing through the branches. From a window a shadowy figure looked out on this garden and, around the edges of the work, somewhat like the decoration one sees in the borders of medieval manuscripts, were objects I recognised: a tortoise paperweight which had held down the plan she'd drawn for our garden, a copy of *Gone with the Wind,* the cup from which I'd had my first taste of green tea, Hanaka's wedding day obi and another book, in Japanese, which I believed to be *The Makioka Sisters*. The final object was a lemon bootee, the same lemon bootee that Divine D knitted for Hanaka's unborn baby.

This work of art told the story, perfectly, of two imperfect lives and of a garden made to its creators' own rules, its glorious 'borrowed landscape' abounding in greater significance in our narrative than even the most revered of pagodas or mountains. The small plaque at the side read *Louise's Garden,* and the date, 1962, proved beyond doubt that Hanaka thought of our time together long after the events which had caused us to be pulled apart.

On that bright Brisbane day, my lost friend handed me a gift that set my spirit soaring: this deeply personal watercolour was Hanaka's loving salute to our friendship.

Made in the USA
Charleston, SC
13 October 2010